Bernice Dueck

Benjamin & Jon

Mary Ellen Heath

Jeremy Books

5624 Lincoln Drive Minneapolis, Minnesota 55436

Jeremy Books

5624 Lincoln Drive Minneapolis, Minnesota 55436

TO GAYLORD

Chapter 1

Benjamin didn't know where he was headed when he first left the Home. He didn't even know whether he was going to stay away for good or come back after a while. He just knew that for right now he had to get away; he couldn't stand it any more.

Right after breakfast he struggled into his jacket, picked up his cane from the corner where it stood, and walked deliberately down the hall and out the door.

Several saw him leave the building, but nobody thought anything about it. They were used to his restless ways, had seen all spring his preference for the patio to the indoor lounge, had watched him pacing about on the handkerchief-sized lawn, stopping at the edge of the flower beds now and then to laboriously bend down and crumble a bit of earth between his fingers or gently nudge a new stalk springing from the ground.

So nobody paid any attention when he went out even though it was early in the morning. They knew that he knew he wasn't supposed to leave the grounds, and he'd never been one to break the rules.

But he did today. In fact, he lay awake last night thinking about it, and had risen early this morning planning to do it. As soon as breakfast was over he started out.

Benjamin was cautious about it though; nobody must catch on to what he was up to. First he made his usual slow circuit of the lawn, examining the progress of each flower and shrub. Then he stopped and sat on the bench at the far corner of the yard, the one nestled against the laurel hedge. While he seemed to rest there he scanned the building, checking every window and every door to see whether anybody was watching. When he was certain that no eyes were upon him, he rose from the bench and stepped around behind the hedge.

That's all there was to it. Benjamin was almost surprised to find it so easily done. He was immediately out of sight of the Home, and his footsteps quickened with eagerness as he stepped onto the sidewalk that headed south straight out of town. He was free. He didn't know how long it would last, but for now at least he was free, his own man once again.

His face turned eagerly to the sky, his practiced eyes taking in the great scope of blue from east to west. Yes, he decided, it's going to be a fine day—a fine day for his leave-taking. He could tell that; there was nothing wrong with his eyesight, whatever else his infirmities might be. So he looked about with pleasure as he stepped sturdily down the walk, joyful with the changing scene. All his cares were soothed away by the balm of the warm sun on his face. Yes, it was going to be a good day.

It was a good day for him, though he grew warm and weary as the morning wore on. Yet if his exuberance faded, his determination did not, and although he had to stop several times to rest—twice sitting on a stone wall, once propped against an old truck—he arose each time and plodded firmly on. Finally, even the sparsely settled fringe of the town was behind him and he found he had reached the west side of the city park.

"Sure is a nice place," he murmured, stopping to rest his gnarled hand against the smooth bark of a young birch as he peered over into the shaded depths of the set-apart place. "A real nice park." He'd seen the outer edges of it innumerable times in the former days, going to and from town. But he'd never stopped and explored any of it, except the northeast corner where the annual church picnic was held. He'd had acres of his own then to tramp around on and hadn't needed a city park. But today it was an enticing place to him, cool with the shade of freshly-grown leaves, lush with a bounty of shrubbery and flowers—a beautiful place. He believed he'd walk over to a bench that stood nearby and rest for a while.

Benjamin left the sidewalk and moved over the uneven ground, remembering to use his cane and lift his feet carefully so as not to stumble over the rough places. Wouldn't do to take a tumble now, just when he'd gotten out on his own again. No, indeed!

He eased himself down onto the hard boards with a sigh of relief and leaned back gratefully. It was good to sit down and relax a bit. He wasn't used to so much walking any more. In fact, for a while he hadn't been able to do any walking at all. His shoulders gave a slight shudder as he remembered the worst days of his illness, but he wasn't going to think about that. He was much better now. Quite able to look after himself, though nobody else seemed to think so. Well, he'd show them!

But right now his weariness would not sustain his anger, so he just rested and looked all about him at the green and growing things, the sights his eyes were hungering for. After a bit his head drooped and he nodded off into a little nap.

Yet though he needed the rest, he couldn't sleep long. He wasn't comfortable enough for that. So after a few minutes he woke with a start and looked about with bewilderment until he recognized where he was and remembered why he was there. And then a surge of anxiety, a fear of the unknown that was before him, caught him unawares and held him for moment. He quickly put it from him, for he'd never been one to tolerate such weakness long. He'd learned better than that back when he was just a young sprout farming his first bit of land. Times were hard then, and he'd learned a man couldn't go around letting fear eat at him, not while there was work to be done and a family to be reared. So it was his habit to meet hard times with courage, and he wasn't going to let down now. Besides, whatever happened to him, it would be better than the Home. So he reasoned his confidence back and stood up from the bench, suddenly very hungry.

"Wonder where I could get something to eat?" he murmured. Then he remembered that there was a refreshment stand near the east entrance to the park, and he headed in that direction, a little unsteady on his feet at first. But after a few steps his balance came back, and he stepped along more firmly.

It was a long way across the park, but after he'd gone half way he spotted the red and white colors of the refreshment stand shining through the trees and angled toward it. Soon he was threading his way through a maze of play equipment, and he stopped for a bit to watch several children scamper and squeal their way from the swings to the teeter-totters to the climbing bars to the slide. How happy they seemed! Carefree and confident, they moved with exuberant assurance through the business of their play. The wiry towhead on the slide could almost have been his son Stephen, and the flying braids on the girl-child who dashed past his feet could have belonged to his own Mary. The pudgy one pumping vigorously in the swing was like Janet.

He didn't look around for a match to Timothy. It was too painful still, even after all these years. You never got over missing one that was gone, it seemed, not one of your own. Oh, you had to put the hard grieving from you, of course, but the loss remained, always there. And the pictures stayed indelible in the mind, the scenes that were too easy to see again. The smashed car, the hospital room, the cemetery with the soft spring rain weeping down. No matter how absent-minded he'd gotten this last year or so, he could never forget those things.

But it was best to put them out of mind and just look at these present children. They were having such a good time that his eyes misted over just from the joy of watching them.

However, right at the moment he needed a meal. No wonder, he noted, glancing down at his watch; it was well past lunch time at the Home. That was one of the aggravating things about the Home—everything had to be done right on schedule. Breakfast, lunch, and dinner, each one had to be eaten at a certain time. Didn't matter how you felt, whether you were hungry or not. Everything had to be done to fit into the routine. No wonder a body's innards got so regulated that they complained if food didn't arrive right on schedule! Well, his stomach would just have to get used to a little freedom from now on!

He approached the refreshment stand and paused at the edge of the trees, studying the group gathered about the place. It wasn't likely anybody there would know him, but you never could tell. People were always turning up in unlikely places, and he didn't want to run into any friends or acquaintances right now. At last, satisfied that he was safe, he marched up and took his place in line, reaching into his pocket to be sure his money was there.

Yes, he had money all right. He'd been saving it up for just such a time as this. He smiled and almost chuckled aloud thinking how surprised Janet would be if she knew how much he had accumulated from the sums of spending money she and Steve had sent him from time to time. He wasn't broke!

He fingered his wallet, then carefully drew it out of his pocket as he moved up a couple of places in the line. Then, as the boy in front of him dashed off with a paper cone filled with purple ice, he found himself face to face with the white-hatted boy behind the counter and knew it was his turn to order.

But to order what? It had been so long since he'd done anything but eat what was put before him that now it was difficult to decide, to tell the boy what he wanted. He studied the menu printed on a big board inside the booth, but none of the words on it seemed to jell into much sense.

"Sir?" The boy under the white cap shifted to lean one arm on the counter. "What'll you have?" Annoyance had crept into his voice, and Benjamin knew he must order. He was holding up the line.

"A hot dog!" he suddenly spluttered. "A hot dog with mustard."

The young man moved deftly, tucking a steaming wiener into a long white bun and cradling it there as he quickly slathered on a generous dab of bright, yellow mustard. Benjamin's mouth watered as he watched. How long had it been since he'd had a good old hot dog like that?

"Here you are, sir." The boy handed him the napkin-wrapped treat and looked at him expectantly. "Anything else?"

There was another embarrassed pause as Benjamin tried to collect his thoughts as to whether he should order anything more.

"Something to drink maybe?" Again came the expectant voice.

"Yes—some coffee." He got that out and then waited awkwardly, hot dog in one hand, wallet in the other, while the boy grabbed a paper cup and then with the flip of a lever splashed in the amber liquid and set it smartly on the counter.

"That'll be ninety-five cents, sir."

Benjamin looked at his wallet in his right hand and his hot dog in his left. Obviously he'd have to put the sandwich down while he got his money out. Carefully he laid the hot dog in its napkin cover on the counter, then turned to his wallet and fished out a one dollar bill.

Benjamin dropped his nickel change in his pocket. Then carrying his hot dog and coffe in trembling hands, he looked for a place to go with them. Not far away he spotted a bench and headed for it. It was shady and quiet there with nobody around. He backed up to one end of the bench and cautiously lowered himself down without spilling a drop. He set the coffee to one side and prepared to start in on the hot dog.

As he lifted the bun to his mouth he looked up and saw with a start that the young man who'd waited on him at the refreshment booth was standing there with an outstretched arm pointing at him, and saying something to two little girls who were also looking in his direction! Had they figured out who he was? Had word gotten around already that he had escaped from the Home? Fear mushroomed with him, pushing up even into his throat as he saw several other people turn to look his way. Then the two little girls came running toward him. He half-rose in panic, thinking he must somehow try to flee.

But it was too late; they were upon him.

"Mister—you forgot your cane!"

"Why—thank you," he managed to get out weakly. "Thanks for bringing it to me."

He took the cane and sank back onto the bench. They smiled shyly at him for a moment, then turned to go. He thought belatedly that he would like to give them something, maybe a dime so they could buy themselves a treat, but before he could speak they were already skipping away.

Benjamin didn't enjoy the hot dog as much as he had anticipated, but he did feel better after getting some food in his stomach. But what about his supper? Maybe he'd better get something to take with him. He'd always relished three square meals a day and didn't care to start doing without now. He rose from his seat and strolled back over to the refreshment booth. It was the first planning he had done since leaving the Home.

This time Benjamin knew what he was going to do and didn't have any trouble. He bought another hot dog and two candy bars and managed to cram them all into his jacket pockets as he turned to leave. He didn't forget his cane this time either, giving it a jaunty swing as he started off again across the park.

Somewhere in the south end of the park was a stream, just a little "crick," as the kids called it. It had been a long time since he'd seen any free-running water—too long. He headed in what he knew must be the right direction and walked a long way down a gently descending slope, then entered a more thickly wooded area. Before him stood a long row of picnic tables and benches that bordered what he thought must be the bank of the stream. His step quickened as he drew near the ragged cleft in the grassy turf of the park, then slowed as he came to the bank's edge. It wouldn't do to step onto a crumbly place and take a tumble. But he found a solid spot and stopped to look, leaning forward carefully as he peered up and down the stream. It wasn't much really, hardly more than a trickle, but the trickle murmured a song as it flowed over and around smooth gray stones and pebbles, and here and there it rang out with a clear, bright sound as it dropped a couple of inches in a miniature fall or squeezed itself together to rush through a narrow strait.

It was music. It was beauty. The moist odor from the damp stream bed was perfume to his nostrils. The old man moved a few steps downstream to a picnic table and sank down on a bench there, weak from the assault of pleasure on his senses. He looked and listened and smelled, feeding his long-starved hungers.

How did they expect a man to live without this? How could he survive encased in four walls and a tiny square of patio and grass? Yet some at the Home didn't seem to mind doing it, at least not like he did. Of course a few were past minding much of anything. But there were others—his friend, Tom Harris, for instance. Tom seemed content enough, at least on the days that he felt good, just visiting and playing checkers and watching television. But then Tom had worked for thirty years in a grocery store, he'd been used to having walls around him all day long and people always underfoot.

All his life, walls had been for shelter at evening, for comfort when rest was due. Not that he hadn't cared about his home. His toil and sweat had gone into building that sturdy, square farm house the first summer after he and Kate were married. It had been a good time for them, working hard together and watching their home rise board by board. Kate had been a wonder, working alongside of him and even clambering up on the roof to nail down shingles. And the house had turned out fine, as solid today as the day it was built. At least he hoped so. It had been a while since he'd seen the place. Surely the Bentons were taking good care of it. He'd hate to think of it getting run down.

But much as he'd cared about his home, it was still just a house. His farm was his love. He'd spent his life on those 160 acres of soil and rock, of trees and waters, of bountiful earth below with an ever-changing sky above.

He could not now endure four walls and a patio.

He rose from the bench after a few minutes and began to make his way downstream. He wanted to explore the little creek. It didn't compare to the one that crossed his farm. It was smaller, muddier, and its banks were trampled by the feet of myriads of picnickers. But it was running water, and he wanted to follow it a ways.

He ambled slowly along the bank, stopping now and then to gaze up and down and across the stream, savoring every scene, until he came at last to a bridge.

It was a small, rustic footbridge, providing access to three picnic tables placed in an inviting glade across the stream. He immediately wanted to cross, for he'd had a weakness for bridges ever since he was a boy. He walked to the near end of it and looked it over. There were no loose boards or steep steps to give him any trouble, so he grasped one handrail firmly and started across. Halfway over, he paused and looked upstream for a long moment. Then he turned and gazed downstream.

He'd always liked the view you get of a stream from right

out over the middle of it. The never-ending flow of waters passed beneath his feet, never to return this way again. There was a hint of mystery to it all that intrigued him.

After a bit, he moved on across the bridge. It was pretty there, the nicest spot he'd found yet in the park. At one edge of the clearing he noticed a faint path leading into a stand of scrubby oak.

"Might as well explore a bit farther," he murmured and set his feet onto the feeble trail. Brush and weeds pressed upon his legs as he waded through, but he kept going. Actually, it felt good to him, this crowding of thick plant growth all about. There was the feeling of wildness here, for apart from the picnic tables in the little glade behind him this part of the park was undeveloped. It was low land; perhaps it flooded in the winter and wasn't worth trying to keep up.

He reached an oak thicket and paused a moment, laying his hand on a low, knobby limb to get the rough feel of it. But the path went on, and he soon followed it. He could not resist. Benjamin was a boy again, and he had to see what was around the next turn of the trail.

He was far out of sight of people now, quite enveloped in the pocket of wilderness. Happily, he savored every rustle of leaf, every insect's hum, and the glory of each shaft of sunlight. He couldn't remember when he'd had such a good time. Not since he'd left his farm, that's for sure. He fervently hoped he'd never get trapped into anything like that Home again.

He'd been sick when it happened and couldn't help himself. The kids had all thought it was the best thing to do. He didn't blame them. None of the three was fixed to care for a sick old man; he knew that, and the last thing he wanted was to be a burden to any of his children. No, he'd had no other choice then but to go into the Home. But now he wasn't sick anymore and he didn't need it. He might be a little weak and wobbly, but he was well enough to look after himself.

How good it was to be doing just that—to be going where he pleased, doing what he pleased.

On and on he trudged, following the path which had returned to and now stayed by the winding stream. At last he found the trail fading away, losing itself in a patch of blackberry brambles that crowded up to the creek bank.

Benjamin hesitated, wondering what he should do next. He supposed he really should turn back. Just then he noticed it—the distinct smell of smoke. It wasn't coming from the picnic area either, but from farther on the brush.

He began to search for a way through or around the blackberry bushes. It seemed hopeless. If he was to go any further, he'd have to cross the creek—and that might not be easy!

Benjamin made his way carefully back along the bank studying the stream with a practiced eye. Ah—there was a shallow place. He couldn't drown himself in that much water even if he fell flat on his face! But he didn't want to fall, and it looked slippery with great, flat rocks most of the way across. Still, if he angled to the left it was gravelly and fairly level. That would be the safest way. But he couldn't walk on that gravel in his bare feet. He'd have to leave his shoes on and get them wet. He hated that idea, but there was no other way.

He took a moment to steady himself and then started across, feeling carefully ahead of each step with his cane.

Finally, he squished one soggy foot out onto the bank before him, grasped a sturdy bush that bent within reach, and hoisted himself out of the water. Then he stood for a moment and rested, gazing down at his wet feet.

This side was steeper than the other, but there were good handholds, so he began working his way up. It was easier than he expected, and in a moment he stood triumphant on a level space at the top of the bank. "I'm not as crippled up as everybody thought," he announced. He sighed as he yearned for the agility of former years. Inside he didn't feel any different from the man he'd been, or even the skinny, shaggy-headed boy before the man. Within him he felt like he could go leaping and running through the woods with never a fear or bother.

But it was a left-over feeling, he knew that. The body that burdened him now was an old man's arthritic frame. It would never do the quick, strong things for him again. Yet it was getting him around today, and he was grateful for that.

Suddenly he was aware that he could now see the thin col-

umn of smoke he could only smell before. It looked like all he
had to do was follow the creek, and it would take him straight
to the fire.

Benjamin's pace quickened as he drew near the last cluster
of bushes that screened the source of the smoke. Then he was
upon it—a campfire. Around a few charred and smoldering
sticks was a carefully arranged ring of rocks, and just beyond,
nestled in a little grove of young oaks, was a crude, lopsided
lean-to.

"Sure as the world, somebody's camping here," he decided.
A fishing pole stood propped against a tree, and beside the fire,
nestled against a log that had been rolled up for a seat, were two
cans of beans and a battered skillet.

"Nice spot," murmured Benjamin. It was private too,
screened behind and on each side by a thicket of brush that
crowded down to the stream edge. And across the creek the
bank was so overgrown that he doubted anyone would ever
penetrate enough to see into this little glade. Even overhead the
oaks stretched out an arbor that partially shaded and concealed.

"Sure takes a body back," he murmured, and he sat for a
while as his mind's eye rambled back through those long ago
days of his boyhood years. He had known good growing-up
years, in spite of all the hard work he'd had to do. How good it
would be now just to be able to turn off a real day's work again!
He'd never been one to want to retire to a rocking chair and
twiddle his thumbs all day. No, he'd kept going as long as he
could, but though the spirit was still willing, the flesh had grown
weak, and now here he was—a hard-working man penned up in
the frame of an old dotard. He was often disgusted with what
his body had become.

Yet today it had served him well enough. Benjamin had
camped out in places like this plenty of times in the past and it
didn't take him long to start thinking about spending the night
right here. Otherwise he had a long hike back. There was the
creek—he'd have to cross that again. And all the brush to get
through. The more he sat and thought about it, the more weary
he became, until he felt it would be just too much effort.

Apparently, whoever had fixed up this camp was not coming

back tonight. Why couldn't he just stay here until morning? He wouldn't bother anything; surely it would be all right.

The excitement of anticipating a real campout again gave Benjamin one more burst of energy. He struggled to his feet and began prowling the outskirts of the campsite for wood. It wouldn't do to use up the supply gathered by the previous occupant; he should get his own.

It was hard work, gathering firewood. He was trembling and sweating in spite of the coming evening chill by the time he decided that he had enough. If his supply didn't last the night, perhaps he could after all use a little of the neat stack beside the fire and then replace it in the morning before he left.

Right now the evening gloom was beginning to descend, so he knew he'd better get the fire rekindled while he could still see what he was doing. He laboriously knelt beside the fireplace and with a stick gently nudged the smoldering coals together in a heap. Then he carefully criss-crossed some tiny dry twigs over them and sat back to watch. In just a few seconds a burst of yellow flame licked up through the twigs, and the fire was going. He gradually added larger sticks until he had a brisk, crackling fire, and the heat of it felt good to him, warming and comforting.

Then he realized he was very hungry again, and thirsty too. He fished the hot dog and a candy bar out of his coat pocket and laid them on the log beside the fire. That would take care of his supper all right, and he'd just have to drink some water from the stream. The hot dog, now cold and greasy in its soggy bun, tasted good to him, and so did the candy bar. He still had the second candy bar tucked away in his pocket, and he debated about eating that too, for he was certainly hungry enough. He decided he'd better save it for morning. The sweet would do for breakfast until he was able to get out and get something more.

Benjamin turned his attention to the lean-to under which he would make his bed. It was a wobbly affair made from poles fastened together with bits of twine and wire, then thatched in haphazard fashion with grass and weeds and leaves. He smiled as he examined the structure. Surely it had been put together by a child, and his curiosity stirred as he wondered about the youngster.

"Sure wouldn't turn much rain," he mused as he poked at the thatching here and there. But it wouldn't rain tonight anyway, and the shelter would do very well as a windbreak. It should also serve as a reflector of heat from the fire nearby, and since he had no cover but his jacket he'd have to depend on the fire and shelter to keep him warm through the night.

He was going to have a hard bed, though. A layer of leaves had been scraped up in the lean-to, but he knew that they weren't going to cushion him very much. Still, it wasn't the first time he'd slept on the ground, and he could surely stand it for one night.

Turning back to the fire, he laid several long-lasting chunks of wood on it, then arranged the remaining limbs close at hand so he could easily feed the fire without having to move far from the shelter.

When he had done all he could for the fire, he let himself down gingerly onto the bed of leaves, stretching his aching legs out slowly one at a time. He'd asked a lot of his creaky old joints this day; they had a right to be sore. After a few minutes of rest the pain let up some, and he sank back more comfortably into his rustling nest. He drew his jacket up tight around his neck to ward off the nighttime chill, and then he lay and stared at the dancing flames until his eyes began to glaze with the coming of sleep.

As he let them close he began a silent prayer, for he was a devout man, and it was his custom to pray to God at the end of his day. But the prayer didn't get very far, for he couldn't stay awake. Yet it didn't matter, for all that he meant to say—all his gratitude for this day of freedom, for being on his own, for finding a small niche of wildness to ease the cravings of his heart—all was there in his simple, "Thank you, Lord . . . "

Chapter 2

Benjamin awoke slowly and painfully the next morning. He wasn't anxious to rouse himself, for somewhere in his not-quite-conscious state he sensed that he was aching all over, and he knew that when he really got awake it was going to hurt like crazy until he'd been up and stirring a while. It was always like that in the morning, and it would probably be worse today. He lay still and tried to doze awhile longer.

As the sunlight poured over the fork of a tree and hit him full in the face, he began to see behind closed eyelids a warm, yellow glow that flashed and flickered with the dancing of the leaves to the morning breeze. He tried squeezing his eyes tighter shut against the bright intrusion, but the effort only woke him further. He gave up and let his eyes open, shifting farther back into the lean-to to escape the glare.

The moment he glanced out of his shelter he was startled wide awake. For there, just beyond the fireplace, a boy stood staring at him.

The boy wasn't doing anything. He just stood there, dangling a rumpled paper bag from one hand and a denim jacket from the other. For a few seconds Benjamin just stared back; then he struggled into a sitting position and gave the boy a sheepish smile. He felt exactly like a small child caught doing something he wasn't supposed to.

"Hello." Benjamin made the first move, but the boy did not respond. He just stood there staring out of a solemn and motionless face.

Benjamin felt he could talk better on his feet, so he grabbed a small tree at one end of the lean-to and began laboriously to lift himself up. It took a great effort, and he nearly groaned aloud with the pain, but he managed to stand upright. Then he turned again to his visitor.

"My name's Benjamin," he said, but again there was no response, just the steady, measuring gaze from the boy's wary eyes.

"Is this your place?" Benjamin continued. "Did you fix it up here, the lean-to and everything?"

After another studying moment the boy nodded. Then, seeming to arrive at some decision, he spoke at last.

"Does this land here belong to you, Mister?"

"No. No, it isn't mine. I think this is still part of the park, although I don't know for sure. I came in through the park anyway, and I never came to any fence marking the boundary of it along the way."

The boy was visibly relieved, and he seemed to relax a bit as he gently set his sack down upon the log and nodded.

"Yeah, I think it's part of the park too, but when I saw you here I wondered if maybe it was yours. Did you sleep there in the lean-to all night?"

"Yes. I hope you don't mind."

"No. It's okay, I guess. I've been wanting to stay here all night myself, but I never get to. I always have to go home."

"Well, it's been a long time since I camped out. But I used to a lot, back when I was your age, or maybe a little older."

"Did you? Whereabouts?"

"Oh, all up and down the river that ran alongside my father's farm down in the southern part of the state. Used to do a lot of fishing, and I'd often camp out all night on the river bank. Sometimes stayed three or four days if I wasn't needed at home."

"Sounds like fun."

"Yes. Yes, it was fun."

There was a moment of silence as Benjamin remembered. Then he noted again the crude fishing pole standing against a tree and gestured toward it.

"Do you like to fish?"

"Yes. Well, I do, but I'm not much good at it. I hardly ever catch anything. Just crawdads sometimes."

"Um-huh—might not be many fish in this little creek. Still, there ought to be a few perch or catfish."

Benjamin picked up the pole and began examining the simple tackle.

"Tell you what, I think you ought to move this sinker up away from the hook a little bit farther. And this fishhook is awfully big for the size fish that you might find around here."

The boy listened with mounting interest.

"Do you think if I had a smaller hook I could catch a fish?"

"Might, if there's any fish here to be caught."

The boy thought for a moment, then came to a quick decision.

"I think I'll try it," he announced with a hint of rising excitement in his voice. "I think I'll go back to town and get some new fishhooks right now."

"Why don't you take this hook along with you to compare," Benjamin suggested, "and get some about half that size."

"Okay, that's a good idea." The boy took a knife out of his pocket and sawed at the line just above the hook until it parted. "There, that does it."

The boy started to leave, taking a few steps down the faint path he seemed to know well, but then he paused and turned a questioning gaze back to Benjamin.

"Are you going to be around here for a while?" he asked.

"Why, yes, I expect I'll still be here when you get back."

The boy hesitated a moment longer as if wanting to ask something more. But he could not quite bring himself to do it.

"Well—I'll see you." He turned and strode into the brush, walking sedately enough at first. Benjamin moved over to where he could watch the departing back, and he was surprised to see the boy, when he thought he was out of sight, spring suddenly into an exhilarated leap down the bank, run churning through the water, and bound exuberantly up the opposite side to disappear into a thicket of willows.

"He's sure in a hurry," Benjamin murmured with a small smile. Well, he understood. He could remember when the prospects of a fishing trip had gotten him all fired up too. He hoped that the boy would catch something now that he'd gotten him all excited with talk about his own exploits. Anyway, he'd enjoy helping the youngster get started. He wouldn't mind wetting a line himself again for that matter.

Just thinking about it started Benjamin peering into the nearby woods to see if he could spot a better pole than the one the boy had been using. It didn't take him long to spy a thicket that offered several prospects.

He grasped one sapling and pulled it apart from the others to look it over up and down. Yes, it was a good one, long and straight with just about the right amount of give.

Cutting the sapling was a tedious task for him. His grasp on the boy's pocket knife was feeble, and he couldn't seem to wield the tool with much force.

"It's a fine thing when a man gets to where he can't even whittle a stick," he grumbled. Yet he wasn't really upset, for it was a satisfying thing to be working on a task he had set for himself.

When he finally got the sapling cut, he carried it back to the campsite and sat down on the log to finish the job, carefully trimming off all the little branches that sprang out from the main stem and cutting off the end at just the right spot. He was just smoothing it down at the large end where the handhold would be when he heard a twig snap and looked up to see the boy coming back. The youngster's movements were restrained now, but Benjamin noticed that his hair, hanging limp and tousled across his forehead, was damp with sweat, and his chest still heaved with the effort to take in enough air to satisfy the demands of his exertions. He hadn't wasted any time, that was for sure.

Benjamin smiled and held out his handiwork.

"Been working on a new pole," he explained and was gratified to see the boy's eyes brighten. It was a considerable improvement over the old one, no doubt about that. It was straighter and lighter and almost twice as long.

"Say, that's neat," the boy murmured, taking the pole and running his hand down the length of it to feel its smoothness. "Really neat."

"Did you find your fishhooks?" Benjamin asked, for the boy carried no package or bundle.

"Oh, sure—here." He reached into his pocket and pulled out a little plastic box. "How do these look? Are they about right, do you think?"

"Yes. Yes, those should do fine."

"I got some new line too," the boy said, reaching into another pocket, "some real fishing line. That other I was using was just some old kite string I had. And here's another float in case I should need it."

"Well, now, it looks like you've got just about everything you need. Shall we get the line on the pole now?"

"Sure." The boy nodded eagerly and began unwinding the line, looking to Benjamin for a clue as to how much to take off the spool.

"That's about enough," Benjamin announced after a moment's judicious eyeing of the uncoiling line. "Now you want to get this end fastened to your pole."

The boy was hesitant about tying on the line, but Benjamin did not do it for him. He showed him how instead. The boy did need help. He did not even know how to tie the line securely and was clearly pleased when after a couple of tries he was able to duplicate Benjamin's demonstration knot.

Then the lesson proceeded to the stretching out of the line to just the right length, cutting it, and fastening on the hook, the sinker, and the float.

"Looks real good," came Benjamin's pronouncement when the boy's half-grown fingers finally completed their last awkward task. He was surprised and gratified to see the pleasure his few words of approval brought to the boy. Hadn't anyone ever told the boy he'd done something well before?

They began to look around for a likely spot to fish and decided to go downstream a ways. But first the boy poked about in a clump of bushes on the bank and drew out a coffee can half full of moist earth and a few feeble earthworms.

"I got these a few days ago, but they're still all right I guess," he ventured, stirring the contents of the can around with his fingers and holding it out for Benjamin to inspect.

"Oughta look good enough to a fish," Benjamin assured him, and, taking up his cane, he began slowly to lead the way. The boy was eager and could easily have run ahead, but somewhat to Benjamin's surprise he held himself back and plodded patiently behind, letting the old man set the pace.

They hadn't far to go to find a spot to try. Benjamin had thought back at the campsite that he could see a deep pool downstream a little way where the creek made a slight bend, and, sure enough, when they reached the place it looked like a good stretch of water. They settled themselves on a grassy bank beside the pool, and in a short time a worm-clothed hook plopped down into the murky depths below, sending circles of waves scudding out to break gently on the far edges of the gravel shore.

Then they waited. Twenty minutes, thirty, an hour maybe. Nothing happened. Not even a nibble. Yet the boy was doggedly patient, not stirring, not speaking, just staring down intently at the bright red float that rested serenely on the placid surface.

"Maybe we ought to move on and try another spot," Benjamin suggested at last. "Doesn't look like there's much doing here."

"Okay," the boy agreed after a bit, though he seemed loath to draw his line from the water and end the chance of enticing some unwary fish that might be ready to bite at just that moment.

But he gave it up, gathered in his line, and they marched off further downstream, the boy falling in behind again and waiting patiently for Benjamin to decide where next to stop.

They soon found another place that looked worthy of a try. Here a big tree jutted from the very edge of the bank, its roots half in, half out of the water, and the base of the tree offered a good place for the boy to sit. When he had settled himself he was instantly intent once more upon watching the activity, or lack of it, of the float upon the water.

Benjamin, seated farther up on the bank, was not so engrossed in the fishing as to fail to notice that his stomach complained increasingly about its lack of breakfast.

He reached into the pocket of his jacket, which he had shed and laid on the bank beside him, and found the candy bar he'd saved. It was a little soft and flattened but still very edible. His mouth watered as he drew it from its wrapping, and he was ashamed of how badly he wanted to just gulp the whole thing down instead of dividing it. He might have done it without the boy even noticing, for the child was too engrossed in his fishing to pay him much heed. Benjamin was almost tempted. Instead, with trembling fingers he broke the bar evenly in half and held out one portion of it in its wrapper to the boy.

"Thanks," he said. Then after pausing a few moments as if thinking whether he wanted to mention it or not, the boy said, "I've got some bread and bologna and a can of pop back at camp. Maybe we ought to stop fishing for a little while and go get lunch."

Benjamin was touched by the youngster's offer, for he knew that the last thing the boy wanted to do was to stop fishing. But he was much too hungry to pass up the opportunity.

"I tell you what," he said, "you stay here and keep fishing, and I'll go back and get the food. Then we can eat right here without interrupting anything."

"Okay, if you don't mind going all that way back. The stuff's in a sack. I set it down somewhere."

"Yes, I remember seeing it."

Benjamin laboriously lifted himself to his feet and trudged back to the camp alone. Once there, he rested a moment, then picked up the bag and started back.

In his eagerness, Benjamin fell. He came down with a thump, and for a moment his breath left him. A great fear came upon him, for he'd been around that Home long enough to know what could happen to old folks with brittle bones broken in a fall. He didn't want to get into that fix.

Then his fear began to give way to anger. "Just a stupid old man," he muttered, castigating himself with the first breath that returned to him. "Just plain stupid."

There was nothing for Benjamin to do but see if he could get up. He maneuvered onto his knees and retrieved his cane. Then, planting the cane firmly before him, he got his right foot underneath him and tried to rise. It didn't work. The cane wobbled too much.

"What I need is to get hold of a good, stout tree," Benjamin murmured. Seeing a young ash down the path a way, he began crawling toward it on his hands and knees, embarrassed and disgusted with himself. "Just like a baby," he accused himself silently. But there was no other way.

A couple of minutes passed while Benjamin rested and worked up his determination for another effort. He began to wonder what he would do if he just couldn't make it. His left knee was feeling weak and sore from a bump it had gotten in the fall. Suppose it wouldn't hold him and he couldn't get up at all. It would be the end of everything for him, all his new-found freedom and independence. He had a brief awful glimpse of being carried back into the Home with a busted-up leg.

He wouldn't think it; he must not be. His knee wasn't that bad, surely. He'd crawled on it; it couldn't be hurt much. It would hold him. Both his legs would hold him; he was sure of it.

He got to his knees again, grabbed a limb as high as he could reach with one hand, and used his cane with the other. Slowly he rose to his feet.

"Good," he murmured cautiously. Yes, it looked like he was going to be able to make it all right. Very slowly he began to move down the path toward the fishing spot.

"Thanks a lot," the boy said with a grin as Benjamin held up the bag of food for him to see. Benjamin realized that it was the first time the child had smiled all day. He was kind of an odd, sober-faced little boy. The smile had opened up for a moment his thin, closed-in face, and Benjamin was glad to see it.

The boy spread the contents of the bag on the grass. There were two slices of bologna, two slices of bread, a banana, and three cookies. Meticulously, he divided the food exactly in half, even down to the odd cookie which he broke squarely in two, and they plunged ravenously into the meal.

Benjamin was surprised at how much better he felt after eating. With his hunger satisifed and his hurts letting up he felt much comforted and relaxed. When the boy returned to his fishing, Benjamin stretched out full length on the grass and drifted off into a nap.

He must have slept a long time, for when he woke the sun had slid a long way down in the sky. As he blinked and stirred, he heard a faint commotion at the water's edge and realized that the noise was what had roused him. Quickly—or as quickly as his stiff joints would allow—he turned on his side and pushed himself up to a sitting position so he could see.

The boy saw him move and turned with an intense whisper.

"I think I almost caught one! It took the float clear under! I could feel it too, but when I went to pull it out it got away."

"Well, now!" Benjamin scrambled closer to the boy so that he could look directly down into the water where fading rings still swept away from the now feebly bobbing float. "At least we know there is a fish in there! Maybe you'll get him the next bite, but first you'd better check your bait."

The boy lifted the pole till the hook emerged from the water, and, sure enough, it was almost bare. Just a shred of worm still hung on it. Quickly he pulled the line in and put a fresh worm on the hook, then eagerly dropped it back into the water. He didn't say a word, but Benjamin could sense his fervent wanting. Benjamin yearned too, for the child.

A long minute went by, then another and another. The boy's eyes were glued to the float, and Benjamin's alternated between the float and the boy's straight, tense back. At times he could almost see in this lad one of his own. It could have been either Steve or Timmy there, for many a time he'd shared a fishing hole with them. Such good times they had then, some of the best times of his fatherhood. None of his own, though, had fished with the urgency of this lad. He wondered why, what reason there was for this boy to want so earnestly to catch a fish.

With the boy wanting it so badly, he wanted it too. He found himself praying for it, for it was his long-time habit to pray about many things, large and small. Yet he wasn't sure this was really the sort of thing one should ask for, so he caught himself and hesitated, pondering the idea.

While he was thinking, the float without even a warning jiggle disappeared, yanked firmly beneath the surface of the water.

"You've got him this time!" Benjamin's excited whisper encouraged the boy as the line whipped straight out towards the opposite bank. "Easy now—don't jerk it—just pull him in easy."

The boy drew the quivering pole up and back till there splashed from the water a twisting catfish. Carefully he lifted the pole higher and to the side until with a final heave he landed the flopping fish safely on the bank.

Seeing the youngster at a loss as to what to do next, Benjamin managed to get hold of the fish and quickly killed it with a blow on a nearby rock. Then he turned it over to the boy and waited patiently as the child struggled to retrieve the hook.

"Now, what do you want to do with it?" Benjamin asked when the boy finally maneuvered the hook free and triumphantly held up his trophy. "Do you want to take it home and have your mother cook it for your supper?"

"No!" The boy shook his head vigorously. "I don't think— she wouldn't want to bother with it. Couldn't we cook it ourselves, over the campfire?"

"Sure, no trouble at all. We'd better get back and get started at it though. It's getting late. Tell you what," he said. "Why don't you go on ahead and get the fire going good?"

"Okay—sure!"

Benjamin's eyes twinkled as he watched the boy dart past him and trot on down the path, his pole clutched firmly in one hand, the fish dangling from the other. Every few steps he turned his head to look down at his catch, and each step he took, every swing of his arms, mirrored his pride.

"Doesn't take much to give the kid a lot of pleasure," Benjamin murmured. A body almost forgot what it was like to be that young, to get so much joy from simple little things. Made it good to be around a younster again, to be reminded.

The fire was crackling briskly by the time Benjamin came in sight of the camp, and the boy was just starting back down the trail to meet him. Benjamin didn't get anxious and hurry this time. He held to his slow, careful pace until he stepped at last up to the log and gratefully eased himself down upon it. Then he showed the boy how to clean the fish, letting the youngster do most of the job, awkward though he was with it.

They had no corn meal to roll it in and no grease for frying, so Benjamin couldn't cook the fish the way he liked, but they put a little water in the skillet so it wouldn't stick and cooked it over the fire. Poached fish, he guessed it was. Anyway, it tasted good to them, and they were both hungry enough to have eaten several fish that size. Benjamin only nibbled at a couple of bites, letting the boy have the pleasure of eating most of his catch.

When the meal was finished they quickly cleaned up, the boy kneeling at the edge of the stream to scour out the skillet with a handful of gravel while Benjamin dug a shallow hole and buried the remains of the fish. When the few chores were done they stood and faced each other awkwardly.

"Well," began the boy, "I guess I'd better be going." He hesitated a moment, then asked, "Are you going to stay here another night?"

"Yes, if it's all right with you, I think I will."

"Oh, sure. It's okay with me."

They stood there for another few moments, and then the boy spoke again.

"Well, what are you going to do for something to eat? The fish wasn't much."

"Oh, it's enough for tonight. If I get hungry I can go get something at the stand over there in the park." Even as he said it, Benjamin realized that his knee was too sore to let him tackle that long, difficult walk this evening. "Tell you what though— are you planning to come back tomorrow?"

"Sure, I come here almost every day."

"Well, maybe I could get you to do a little shopping for me on the way?"

"Sure."

Benjamin drew out his wallet and carefully fished out a couple of dollar bills.

"How about getting me a loaf of bread and a pound of bacon? And maybe some fruit, two or three bananas or apples or whatever looks good. If there's any change left over, get yourself a candy bar or something."

"Okay." The boy pocketed the money and turned to go. But as he reached the edge of the clearing he suddenly stopped and turned back.

"I almost forgot to tell you," he announced, "my name's Jon."

"Well, I'm glad to know you, Jon."

"Yeah. Well, I'll see you."

"Yes—so long, Jon."

Kind of a funny little fellow, Benjamin thought as he watched the boy go trudging off through the woods. Hard to imagine a youngster catching his first fish and not wanting to take it home to show his folks. He could remember how proud his boys had been of their first catches. They'd worn him and Kate out telling about it.

Maybe there was some reason this one didn't want his folks to know what he'd been up to. He stirred uneasily, for he hoped he hadn't been encouraging the boy to disobey his parents. Maybe he'd better look into that tomorrow. Could be the kid was supposed to stay home today instead of out roaming around on his own. Some parents were pretty fussy about knowing their children's whereabouts, and Jon hadn't even gone home for lunch. Yes, he'd better question the boy about it, if he really did come back tomorrow. Might be he'd change his mind in the morning and decide he didn't want to spend the day hanging around with an old man. Might be he'd even decide to take that two dollars and do something with it besides buying groceries. Benjamin didn't think it would turn out that way. Jon seemed like a good boy, one who would do what he said.

They had had a good time today, no doubt about that, and they'd gotten on very well after the first little bit. Maybe it was because of the difference in their ages, for if there were things the child was too young to do, there were also things the man was too old to do, and it put them on a rather equal footing.

Yes, Benjamin thought, the boy would be back.

Chapter 3

It was late in the morning when Benjamin heard the snap-ping of a twig and looked up to see the boy emerge from the leafy thicket into the open campsite.

"Hello!" Benjamin's relief came out in a hearty greeting and wide smile, for he had begun to worry some. Still, he chided himself, he shouldn't have expected the kid to show up at the crack of dawn when probably there were other things he had to do first, like chores at home.

"Hi." Jon returned the greeting with a little grin, but he seemed very reserved, almost embarrassed. He stopped at the edge of the woods and hesitated to approach further, although it seemed obvious that the grocery bag he held high in his arms contained the foodstuffs Benjamin had ordered.

"Got my groceries?" Benjamin queried, and then there was nothing Jon could do but bring them forward. When he handed over the sack, so tall it had shielded the side of his face, Benja-min saw what the trouble was. The boy was sporting a black eye. Why he was embarrassed about it, Benjamin didn't know. When he was a kid, Benjamin had always been kind of proud of the bumps and bruises he'd gotten.

"Quite a shiner you've got there," he commented, deciding it would be better to mention it right away than to try to ignore something so obvious. Maybe if he treated it lightly the boy would get over his embarrassment. "Who won—you or the other fellow?"

"It wasn't a fight or anything like that." The boy's head turned away, and Benjamin was surprised to see his mouth tremble. "It was—something else—an accident."

It was plain that for some reason Jon was ashamed of the black eye and didn't want to talk about it, so Benjamin quickly turned his attention to the sack of groceries. He was hungry, and the bacon sandwich he prepared turned out to be the best thing he had tasted in a long time. He tried to share his bacon with the boy, but Jon refused, wasn't hungry he said. He just sat, hunched up on the log, waiting patiently for Benjamin to finish his meal.

"Planning to do some fishing again today?" Benjamin asked.

"Yeah, I thought I would." A spark of life came into the boy's voice again, and he went to retrieve his pole from the tree against which it had stood since last evening.

"Maybe I'll give it a try too," Benjamin said. He was surprised with the glad response that swept the boy's face. Seemed strange the kid was so happy to be doing things with an old man. Well, Benjamin was glad for the welcome to his offer of companionship anyhow, and the two were quickly engaged in the search for another good fishing pole.

The fishing started off slowly again, but it didn't seem to matter so much. The boy was eager but not anxious this time. Benjamin guessed he'd done his proving yesterday; today he could be more relaxed about the whole thing. So they sat on the bank, Jon in his spot of previous success and Benjamin a few feet downstream, and they fished away the day. Sometimes they talked. Sometimes they just silently took in the comfort of the sun and the relief of shade when the sun grew too warm, felt the gentle touch of passing breezes, watched the tranquil flow of the waters. It was a good time.

"Your Dad ever take you fishing?" Benjamin asked when Jon had settled back after a futile flurry of nibbles.

"No."

"Not much of a fisherman, eh?"

"Well, he does go fishing once in a while. He has friends—guys he does business with—and sometimes they fly somewhere and go fishing. I think it's in Canada. But it's just men—they don't take any kids along."

"Well, maybe some time when you get more grown up he'll take you with him." Benjamin was sorry now he'd brought it up. But he had learned something about Jon's father. Apparently he was a man who had time for fancy fishing junkets with business associates but none for spending on a creek bank with his son. A strange set of priorities, but some fathers were like that. Not Benjamin, though. He'd never gotten too busy to spend plenty of time with his kids. He was glad he had all those good times to look back on, though the memories were bittersweet, for he couldn't relive the fishing trips, the campouts, the hikes, without stirring up a yearning to have his children back again. What a good family they'd been! But now his children were grown up and so preoccupied with their own affairs that their lives only touched his lightly it seemed. He still missed his little folks.

Well, that was the way of things, and he certainly wouldn't have wanted to keep them young forever. And since he could no longer be father to little ones of his own, perhaps he could at least be something to this boy, for he was beginning to suspect that Jon needed somebody to take an interest in him.

"What kind of work does your father do, Jon?"

"Oh—I don't know exactly. He has an office downtown. And he's gone a lot. He's usually home on weekends though. But even then he sometimes has a lot of work to do."

So, it was the old story, Benjamin decided. A classic case of a businessman too wrapped up in his affairs to pay any attention to his family. Still, he shouldn't pass judgment too quickly. Jon might be exaggerating. Kids sometimes did that, especially if they were peeved at their parents about something. Or the man might be in a situation where he couldn't help himself for some reason.

Whatever it was, the boy was suffering from it, and no wonder. Growing up wasn't the easiest thing in the world at best, and if a kid weren't getting plenty of help from his parents it could be awfully hard.

As he sat philosophizing about child-rearing and chiding himself with a little chuckle about how easy it was to see just where the other fellow was going wrong, he was startled from his reverie by the sight of his float taking a quick dip under the water.

"Got one," he announced needlessly when he looked up to

see Jon standing before him with a grin stretched from ear to ear. "Now it's your turn."

Jon crouched to admire the catch a minute, but then he quickly returned to his own pole. As luck would have it, he did have a turn next. Scarcely five minutes went by before he pulled in a catfish, smaller than yesterday's but big enough to eat. Then a flurry of nibbles kept them excited for another hour until Benjamin finally caught one more. After that their luck ran out, and they sat quietly on the bank as their exuberance slowly faded.

"Want to cook the fish in camp again?" Benjamin asked at last.

"Sure."

"Well, I expect we'd better call it quits then and get to cleaning them."

"Okay." Jon was obviously reluctant to quit fishing, but he didn't try to argue, and after a moment he pulled in his pole.

They gathered up their gear and made their way back to camp, where Benjamin built up the fire while Jon struggled with the task of cleaning the fish. Benjamin kept an eye on the operation, but he let the boy do all the work himself, and he was pleased to see the satisfaction with which Jon finally laid the three fish out on a smooth end of the log.

"They're ready," he announced.

"You want to cook them too?"

"Sure."

Benjamin got the skillet and carefully lifted out a leaf and a twig that had blown into the bacon grease left over from his morning meal. The fish would be a lot better to his way of thinking fried in this grease than poached like the one they'd cooked yesterday. He carefully propped the skillet over the fire, and soon the fish were sizzling side by side in the pan.

After dinner, Jon, seeming eager to help, scurried about burying fish scraps, scouring the skillet, and gathering a new supply of wood. Nothing was said, but both took it for granted that Benjamin would stay the night again.

Then, when there seemed to be nothing left to do, Jon began gathering armloads of leaves and grass to add to the bed under the lean-to. He searched here and there in the woods, looking for any materials that would be good to pile onto the heap.

Benjamin was touched with the boy's concern for his comfort, but he began to grow uneasy as darkness approached and Jon showed no signs of leaving for home. The boy kept puttering about, even after he had cushioned the bed to his satisfaction, finding other little things to do about the camp, postponing his leave-taking as long as possible it seemed.

Finally Benjamin decided he's better say something.

"Jon, it's getting pretty late—don't you suppose your folks are expecting you home by now?"

"Oh, they don't care as long as it isn't real dark by the time I get in."

"Don't they expect you for supper?"

"Naw, it doesn't matter. Lots of times I eat out here or get me a hamburger on the way home."

Benjamin pondered that for a moment. What a strange way for a family to behave, not even caring enough to gather themselves together at meal times. A picture of his own happy brood clustered around the family table flashed through his mind. They'd had a lively time over their meals too, talking and laughing, teasing a little now and then. There had been good times around their table, and it had been a rule that when meal time rolled around, everyone had to be there unless there were some mighty good reason not to be.

Things were evidently different around Jon's home.

"Are you sure," he pressed, "that your mother doesn't mind your being away all day like this? Does she have any idea where you are?"

"Oh, yes, she knows I go to the park a lot. It's fine with her. It keeps me out from underfoot, she says." Then a sudden suspicion seemed to cross the boy's mind, for he darted a sharp glance at Benjamin, then looked away. But after a moment he spoke out his doubt.

"Do you mind me hanging around here? Am I getting in your way or anything?"

"Heavens, no! You've been a big help to me, bringing me groceries and everything. And besides I'm glad for the company." Benjamin hoped he was being reassuring without gushing. It was true, he did need the boy's help. Maybe it would be good to let him know that.

"Tell you what—can you come back tomorrow?"

"Yes, I thought I would."

"Well, could I get you to buy me some more things?"

"Sure."

"Okay, good." Benjamin rattled off a list, gave the boy some money, and watched him disappear again down the trail.

When all was silent, Benjamin sank down on the log to rest and take in the coming of the evening.

Then it occurred to him that it seemed to be getting dark awfully early. Could it be clouding up? He looked overhead and saw the fading sky was clear, as it had been all day. Yet the dusk bore an ominous amber tinge that he recognized. He rose from his seat and moved down to the stream where an opening between overhanging branches let him peer into a wider stretch of sky. Sure enough, there in the south and west was building up a thunderhead of black, heavy clouds. Even as he watched he saw faint flicker of lightning, and a long moment later heard the rumble of distant thunder. The storm would come his way, not much doubt of that. The prevailing winds were nearly always out of the southwest this time of year.

Still, it might not amount to anything. Often these early summer storms were just fuss and bluster and little else. Anyhow, there was nothing he could do but wait it out and see. He sighed and made his way back to the fire, for already a cool breeze, flung from the distant cloud heaps, had laid a warning chill upon his shoulders.

He wondered if he had enough firewood to get him through the night and peered anxiously at the stack arranged beside the fireplace. Yes, Jon had dragged up a good supply. His heart warmed as he viewed the evidence of the boy's concern. The little tyke had done a lot to try to make him comfortable, and it was all unsolicited favor. He sure seemed like a thoughtful boy.

Benjamin pulled a couple of big chunks into the fire to build it up for a little more warmth. Then he ducked into the lean-to and, wrapping his jacket snugly around his shoulders, burrowed down into the mound of leaves heaped there. The bed was softer since Jon had added more leaves and grass, and Benjamin soon fell asleep.

For a long while he slept, on into the wee hours, knowing nothing more of the gathering storm. But at last when the wind struck hard into the moaning, twisting trees about him he awakened and rose to peer out of his skimpy shelter. At first all was blackest black except for the fierce glowing of campfire coals fanned to shining brightness by the wind. Then the darkness was split by a flash of light followed quickly by a crash of thunder.

All was silent for a long moment as if even the wind had been subdued by the shock, but then came another blast of light and sound, and with it the air exploded again into sweeping, tearing gusts of wind.

The lean-to stirred and trembled as the two trees which supported it swung to and fro. Though it pulled and creaked against its bindings, the little structure held intact, but much of the thatching was torn loose. When the rain swept in on the heels of the wind there was little protection left for the old man huddling there.

Benjamin could do nothing but endure. He drew his jacket over his head and shoulders and crouched back into what seemed the most sheltered corner, but even that spot was soon drenched by flying spray and dribbles leaking through the tattered roof. By the time the brash, blustering storm had passed he was soaked to the skin.

It wasn't a very cold night. Even so, wet through like he was, Benjamin shivered whenever any slight breeze turned his clinging garments into a skin of ice. Soon he was chilled to the bone, but there was nothing he could do about it except sit and shake, for the fire was out, drowned by the downpour, and there was no dry, warm place for him anywhere.

After a bit, when he was sure the rain was over, he crept out of the lean-to and made his way over to the log. There he sat, hunched toward the fireplace, unknowingly seeking the aura of heat and comfort that usually emanated from it. It was the best he could do for himself, and it was nothing at all.

After a while, Benjamin could scarcely think of any other time than this stretch of dark, wet night. When had the shining sun ever spread its blanket of light over him and tucked its warmth around him? The world was only dark and cold, and he could not seem to think of it as ever being anything else.

At last the reaching fingers of dawn lifted the night's curtain enough to let a sliver of light slip through and spread up into the eastern sky. Morning soon followed, and just as the first rays of sunlight came seeping through the trees Benjamin heard the tell-tale rustle that heralded someone's approach.

He could hardly believe that Jon had gotten here so early, but there he was, laden down with a blanket, a towel, a thick terrycloth robe, and a wad of newspapers.

"You got pretty wet last night, huh?" came the sympathetic query.

"Yes—pretty wet."

Benjamin started to wrap the blanket around him, but then hesitated, for his clothes were still wet. "Guess I'd better get out of these things first," he said, and he handed the blanket back to Jon to hold while he stripped off his wet garments. Then, trembling with the chill from the damp breeze that swept down into the glade, he put on the robe, clutched the blanket tightly around him, and sank down on a pad of dry newspapers that Jon had spread for him on the log. And there he sat, shaking but warming, as the boy scurried about getting a fire made.

The wood was wet on the outside but dry within, so when Jon carefully criss-crossed some branches over a heap of crumpled newspapers they sputtered and steamed only a few moments before catching. As the fire blazed up, Benjamin hunched forward to soak up its warmth.

Meanwhile Jon bustled about doing other chores. First he gathered up Benjamin's clothes and spread them out on nearby bushes. "They'll dry pretty quick when the sun gets to them," he said. Then he peeled a half dozen slices off the bacon and stretched them out to fry in the skillet.

Soon they were both eating bacon sandwiches, and Benjamin suspected from the gusto with which Jon consumed his that the boy had left home without any breakfast. It bothered him some, wondering whether Jon's mother knew, and if she did what she thought about it, but he decided not to ask any more questions now.

Benjamin swallowed the last bite of his sandwich with a sigh of immense satisfaction. What a boost that hot bacon and bread was! It warmed him inside while the blanket and fire warmed him outside. He wasn't really cold any more, but his body still gave an involuntary shudder now and then, so he remained hunkered over the fire, soaking up the heat.

"I couldn't buy any groceries on my way over," Jon said after a bit. "The stores weren't open yet. But I'll go back pretty soon and get some stuff."

"Well, there's no hurry—I'm pretty full right now."

"Yeah. Me too."

There were a few minutes of silence, and Benjamin was sinking into drowsiness when Jon's voice broke abruptly into his consciousness. "I happened to watch the news on TV last night."

Benjamin looked up to see Jon staring intently at him, ready with something more to say, but waiting first for some response. But what was there to say, what had the TV news to do with him? Still, he tried to gather his thoughts to make some answer.

"Anything interesting on?"

"Well—one thing I wanted to ask you about."

"Yes?"

"Well, it seems that there's this man who went off and left some nursing home, and they don't know where he is. They're looking for him. His daughter came here to try to find him too. They said on TV his first name was the same as yours—Benjamin. Benjamin Wright, they said it was." Jon hesitated and looked away for a moment. Then he got his courage up and went on again. "Would that by any chance be you?"

So, he was caught. He might have known there would be a fuss made when he disappeared from the Home. To think it had even been on television!

He looked at Jon and saw the question still holding in the boy's eyes.

"Yes," he sighed at last. "I guess I'm the one they're looking for." Then he turned the questioning to Jon. "Are you going to say anything to anybody about it? About knowing where I am?"

Jon turned his eyes away and shrugged. "I don't know," he said. They sat in silence for a minute, and then Jon spoke again.

"Why did you leave that place anyway?"

"It just got so I couldn't stand it there any longer."

"Were they—mean to you or something?"

"Oh—no, not exactly. Most of them meant well enough, I guess." He stopped and fumbled about in his mind trying to find exactly what it was that was so bad about the Home. Then he spilled it out.

"It's a prison! The place is a prison, that's what!" He was surprised at the bitterness in his voice. He hadn't meant to unload on the boy so hard as that. He quieted his tone and spoke again. "It's just like being caught in a trap. I need . . ." He hesitated, groping again for words. "I just can't stand it—being cooped up like that."

Again there was a long moment of silence, and then Jon spoke his decision.

"Well, I won't say anything about it to anybody. Only there is one thing. That woman—you know, your daughter—I think she is pretty worried."

"Yes, I suppose so." He might have known his kids would get upset when he disappeared like that. He should have let them know, he guessed, and wondered why he hadn't thought about it before. But now what could he do about it? Should he go back just so as not to worry them? No! The rebellion within him rose up stronger than the compassion he felt for his children. He wanted to save them from worrying about him, but not at the cost of returning to the Home. There must be some other way. He stirred the problem around for a few minutes, and then it came to him what he could do.

"I guess maybe I'd better write her a letter," he announced. "Could you get me some paper and an envelope and a stamp, do you suppose?"

"Sure. I can get it when I go for the groceries." Relief came into Jon's voice. "They've got paper and stuff like that at the store. And I can mail it for you when you get it done too."

Benjamin could see that Jon was glad to have the problem worked out, and he was happy to have his own burden of guilt eased. He didn't want to worry his children, but he didn't want to spend the rest of his days in the Home either. So he'd write and let them know he was okay and tell them not to worry or bother about him any more.

Jon began moving about the campsite, building up the fire for more heat, then raking the leaves out of the lean-to and spreading them to dry. He paused now and then to study the shelter and assess the damage done. It was plain that he was dissatisfied with it, but he said nothing, only squinted his eyes with the figuring that went on inside his head.

When all the chores were done to his satisfaction he glanced up to measure the sun's position and turned again to Benjamin.

"I expect the stores are open by now. I'd better go buy our groceries. Is everything okay here until I get back?"

Assured that it was, the boy was swiftly gone, and Benjamin relaxed in the quiet of the fresh-washed woods and the increasing warmth of the summer day.

When Jon got back with the supplies, he found the old man still resting.

"Well, here are the groceries," the boy announced, setting a bulging bag down in the shade of a dense clump of oak sprouts. "And here's some paper and some envelopes." He handed over a tablet of lined paper and a packet of envelopes, then reached down into the grocery bag, feeling for something else. "Here," he said, drawing out a bright red ballpoint pen, "I brought you a pen to write with too. I didn't know if you had one or not."

"Thanks. It's a good thing you thought of it. I don't believe I have one with me."

Jon seemed proud to receive the little compliment, and he stood still for a moment with a pleased look on his face. Then he dived back into the bag and pulled out another package, a shiny plastic square.

"I got this to make our lean-to more waterproof," he explained.

"What is it?"

"It's what they call a ground cover. You know, one of those

big sheets of plastic that people take to put down on the ground under their sleeping bags when they go camping." Jon pulled the plastic sheet out of its wrappings and began unfolding it. "It's pretty big, see? We can spread it out over the lean-to and tie it down at the corners, here where the metal rings are. And I bet that'll fix it so you won't get wet next time it rains."

For a moment Benjamin was speechless. To think that the boy had figured this all out! And gotten the plastic sheet all on his own!

"Well!" he managed to say finally. "Thanks! Thanks a lot. That looks like it just might work out fine."

They carried the bulky sheet around to the back side of the lean-to and carefully spread it out. Yes, it looked big enough to cover the little shelter. They checked the frame of the lean-to and whittled off several sharp twigs that were sticking up where they might punch holes in the plastic. Then they drew the sheet up over the structure. When it was positioned squarely across the frame Jon cut some pieces of twine and tied each corner down securely.

"That should do it," he announced, standing back to view the results of his labor. "I bet that'll turn water the next time we have a storm."

"Looks good," Benjamin agreed. "Now if I just had a shovel so I could ditch it."

"Ditch it?"

"Yes. If we had a little ditch all around the edge of the lean-to we could drain the water away so it wouldn't run in."

Jon stood silent, taking the idea in, and Benjamin could see the wheels turning in the boy's head as he studied the shelter area.

"Usually people make a ditch like that around their tents when they go camping," Benjamin explained further.

"Yeah, it sounds like a good idea. And all we need is something to dig with, right?"

"Yes."

"Well, I'll go see if I can find some sharp rocks to try."

The boy bounded off toward the creek bank to search for digging tools before Benjamin could remonstrate that it would be too difficult a task without a real shovel. Then, as he peered down at the earth and scuffed at it a bit with the toe of his shoe, he began to think that maybe it wouldn't be too hard, for the soil was still moist from the rain and fairly loose where over the years it had absorbed layer after layer of rotting oak leaves.

When Jon came back bearing two flat stones, each with a fairly sharp edge, Benjamin took one without protest, knelt, and began to dig into the moist, dark loam.

It was hard work. The boy was awkward because of his youth, and the old man was slow because of his age, so in this task they were evenly matched. Yet tedious though the work was, they pushed the ditch along until it stretched across the front of the lean-to, then down each side, and finally they were at the back working toward each other from the corners. They worked silently, for the chore took just about all their energy and left little for talking.

Finally they met, heads almost bumping, and joined their shallow ditches to complete a square trench running all the way around the shelter.

"Now," breathed Benjamin with a sigh of satisfaction, "we must put in a ditch to drain all this. Let's run it from that front corner. See, it's all downhill from there; should let the water run off all right."

"Okay. I'll start."

"It doesn't need to be very long. Just dig it far enough to get the water headed away from the campsite. We don't want a gully washer running right down through the camp!"

Jon hopped up and transferred his efforts to the drainage ditch. Benjamin didn't try to help; he knew he was about played out for right now.

They'd done a good job, he decided, eyeing what he could see of the shallow ditch. With the help of this eager youngster he was going to be fixed up comfortably. Benjamin wondered again about Jon, why the youngster was willing to spend so much time with him. Surely he must have other friends, other interests. Yet Benjamin was glad to have his company for as long as the boy desired to give it. He guessed he'd have been in kind of a fix without Jon.

"When are you going to write that letter to your daughter?" the boy's voice suddenly piped to him from beyond the lean-to.

"Oh—I guess I'd better get at that pretty soon."

"I'll bring you the paper and stuff."

Benjamin started to get up but then slumped back down again. He could write the letter right here as well as any place. He kind of dreaded starting it. It would be hard to know just what to say.

"Here you are." Jon laid the tablet and envelope in his lap and handed him the pen. "When you get it done I can take it and mail it this afternoon, and it'll probably be delivered tomorrow. Then that lady—your daughter—won't be worried any more."

"Yes. We'd better try to get it in the mail today."

Benjamin opened the front flap of the tablet and stared down at the fresh, blank paper. How should he start it? Well, first of all, the date.

"What day is this, Jon?" he called to the boy, who was back at work on the drainage ditch.

"Uhm—Thursday."

"I mean what day of the month."

"Oh. I don't know. All I remember is today's Thursday."

"Well, that's enough, I guess."

Slowly and carefully he wrote the word "Thursday" in the upper right hand corner of the paper. She'd know well enough from that when the letter had been written. Then moving his hand over to the upper left he got down "Dear Janet." But it took some studying before he could get in mind what to say after that. Finally, though, his hand moved down to another line, and he began his message.

"I have left the Home. I don't mean to complain, but it just isn't a good place for me to be. I am well enough to look after myself now, so there is no reason for me to stay there any longer. I hope you won't worry about me. I am fine. I have a friend who helps me out when I need it. Tell Steven and Mary you have heard from me. I will write you again one of these days so you will know I am okay.

Much love,
Dad"

There, it was done. He swept a critical eye across the page. His handwriting could be better, but at least it was legible, and that was more than he could have said during the worst of his illness. He'd gotten so he couldn't even sign his name for a while, and that had made him feel pretty helpless. But now, though it wavered a bit, the handwriting was plain enough to read without difficulty.

He tore the sheet of paper gently from the tablet and laid it to one side. Now he must address the envelope. He'd have to be careful with that. Maybe it would be best to print it.

Breathing heavily, he bent again to his task, and the letters went onto the envelope one by one till the three lines of name and address were complete. He folded the letter once, twice, and once again, tucked it down inside the envelope, and licked the flap to seal it shut.

He leaned back with a sense of accomplishment. Now his son and daughters would know that he was all right. He needn't be concerned that he was worrying them.

As he sat there resting in the warm sun, everything else seemed to be all right too. The shelter was fixed up. He didn't need to worry about spending another miserable night like the last one. He had plenty to eat and a blanket to keep him warm. All about him was the grace and beauty of trees and sky and a bit of water—and he had a friend.

What more could an old man want?

Chapter 4

The days passed quietly and peacefully, becoming a week, then two weeks. Each day the boy came to the old man bringing food and drink and often something extra. He had found a thrift shop along his route and added two plastic plates, a saucepan, a handful of bent silverware, two heavy mugs, and a battered coffee pot to their collection of camping gear.

One day Jon showed up with a brand new hatchet to cut firewood. Benjamin had argued about that purchase, insisting that it was too expensive for Jon to buy with his own money. He tried to reimburse the boy. After all, he argued, he was getting the most good from the fire, since he remained in the camp overnight, so it was only fair that he pay for the hatchet to chop the wood.

But the boy was adamant. He'd wanted a hatchet for a long time, he said; he'd been planning to get it before Benjamin ever came to his camp. It was his money, and this was what he wanted to spend it on. Benjamin at last gave up trying to pay and let Jon have his way.

The tool was a big help to them in preparing their firewood, for this was getting to be a bigger chore all the time. They had used every scrap of material to be found close by, and each day they had to range a bit farther to find limbs and branches to drag back to the campsite. Jon did most of this work. He could scamper about through the woods making three trips back and forth to Benjamin's one, but Benjamin helped as well as he could. And when it came to wielding the hatchet, he was much more adept than Jon. Not for nothing had he chopped cord upon cord of wood each winter until the year he and Kate had finally bought an oil heater and an electric range. If there was one thing he knew how to do, it was to chop wood.

Jon was getting the hang of it too, but one day when Benjamin handed him the hatchet, Jon winced as he took it. He shifted it to his left hand and began awkwardly hacking at a big oak limb he had dragged up. Chopping left-handed was awkward for him, and after a couple of minutes Benjamin couldn't resist intervening.

"Got a sore arm?" he asked.

"Yeah."

"What's the trouble? Anything serious?"

"Naw. I just—twisted it or something."

"Well, why don't you let me finish cutting the wood today. It's pretty hard doing it that way."

"Well—okay."

Benjamin took the hatchet back and briskly went about finishing the task, saying no more about the sore arm. Funny how reticent the boy was about his hurts. He sure seemed to be accident prone. First there had been that black eye. Then three or four days ago he'd showed up with a cut and swollen lip. Benjamin had ignored that. Now, he had a sore arm. Strange, the boy didn't appear to be clumsy around camp. In fact, he hadn't gotten so much as a scratch the two weeks they'd been knocking about in the woods together. But he was sure getting banged up somewhere. Well, that was a boy for you. Benjamin could remember when he'd collected a lot of scrapes and bruises himself. One summer he'd kept his mother busy bandaging his wounds, and then he'd finished the season by breaking his arm the day before school started. That's the way it went sometimes.

Jon was sitting down beside the stream when Benjamin chopped the last limb in two and tossed it onto the woodpile. He just sat there staring into the water, now and then flicking a pebble from his fingers out into the water to make a tiny splash. As Benjamin watched, not knowing whether to intrude on the boy's private moment or not, Jon suddenly grabbed up a big rock and flung it across to the opposite bank, where it landed with a tumbling crash. The quiet that succeeded the commotion seemed to call forth something more from the boy, and he sprang to his feet and searched out another stone, which he threw even harder than the first. A third followed, and a fourth, and then the child exploded into a frenzy of rock throwing. It was as if he were trying to stone to death a clump of brush and fern that clung to the edge of the bank. Suddenly the fury ended, and Jon sagged against a nearby tree, clutching his right elbow in his left hand. He'd used his sore arm to hurl the rocks, and it must be hurting even more now.

"Something's really got him upset," Benjamin told himself, but he didn't interrupt the spasm of rock throwing, for he guessed that Jon needed to let off steam. But when the boy had quieted and slumped back to the ground, Benjamin went over and sat down beside him.

"Something wrong, Jon?" he asked after a moment.

"No!" But the boy's face twisted and gave away the lie. Benjamin reached his hand out to touch Jon's shoulder then, and after a quivering instant of hesitation the child tumbled weeping into his arms. Though he wept and trembled he would give no word of the reason for his tears. He kept his cries soft and smothered as if he had long ago learned to hold them in.

"Not like my children," Benjamin told himself. "When they cried about anything they usually squalled good and loud."

This child was different. He'd given way momentarily, but he was already trying to stifle his sobs, and then he began pulling away in shame from Benjamin's comforting hold. Benjamin let him go but remained sitting close by. When the boy was quiet and still he spoke again.

"Jon, is there anything wrong that you'd like to tell me about? Anything I can help you with?"

The boy's back stiffened, but no words came out. Benjamin tried again.

"Is it something I've done that's bothering you?"

"Aw, no!" came the quick, almost angry response. "You haven't done anything. You've been . . . " The voice quavered and stopped, and Benjamin could tell the boy was struggling to hold back the tears. Well, best just let the matter rest for now, he decided. Obviously Jon didn't want to talk about whatever was wrong, and he didn't believe in pressing a child too hard. Better to change the subject and talk about something else.

"You know," he said, getting up and walking a few steps away, "I think I'm going to have to get into town pretty soon.

Thre's some shopping I sure need to do."

After a moment the boy scrambled to his feet and followed, although now his embarrassment kept him at a distance from the old man.

"What kind of shopping?" he asked. "Haven't I been getting you all the stuff you need?"

"Oh, yes. You've been doing a good job, but there are a few things I need to pick out for myself. A razor, for instance, and some clothes."

It was true. He had thought at first that he'd just grow a beard and not be bothered with shaving, but the scratchy stubble on his face bothered him, made him feel disheveled and untidy. He'd always been a clean-shaven man, and he decided he wanted to stay one.

Then there was the problem of his dirty clothes. Without something to change into, it was hard to do without them long enough to get them washed. What he needed was a complete change of clothes.

"Well, when do you want to go?" asked Jon.

"What would you think about today?"

"Okay by me." Jon shruggedand shifted his weight hesitantly from one foot to the other. "Do you want me to go along?"

"I sure do. Don't know how I'd get along without you."

"Okay. Shall we start now?"

"Might as well, I guess."

Benjamin headed for the path by which he had first entered the campsite. Then he paused and turned back to Jon. "Why don't you lead the way? Maybe you know a better way out of here than I do."

"Okay." Jon led off, proud to have a bit of expertise to demonstrate. Upstream from the spot where Benjamin had made his original crossing, Jon stopped. "This is the easiest place to cross," he explained as he left the path and began descending a gentle slope down to a sandy bar. "See, it's real smooth all the way across and not very deep either."

With one hand wielding his cane and the other clamped onto Jon's shoulder, Benjamin stepped steadily across the stream with no difficulty.

"Well, that wasn't much trouble," he said with a grin after they had crossed the stream easily. "You picked a good spot all right."

With the hurdle of the crossing out of the way it didn't take long, even at Benjamin's deliberate pace, to make their way through the remaining woods and into the wide expanse of the park. After being enclosed in the tight-woven thickets for so long, Benjamin felt exposed and conspicuous out in the open. Not likely he'd be recognized though. Most of his old friends and neighbors came into town on Saturdays to do their trading. Still, you never knew. He'd better get this little shopping expedition over with and get safely back into the woods again. His hideaway had begun to feel like home to him.

With Jon guiding the way, the pair went first to a drug store where Benjamin bought a safety razor and some shaving cream. That done, a surge of confidence filled him. He could take care of his affairs all right; he was doing fine.

"Where do you want to go now?" Jon asked.

"Well, I used to buy my work clothes over at Middleton's. But that's quite a ways from here, isn't it?"

"Yes, but we can take the bus right to it."

"Well—do you know where to catch the bus?"

"Sure, right down there at the end of the block."

Thirty minutes later they stood in front of the big department store. Benjamin pushed confidently through the door and headed for the elevator. He knew his way around this store; for he'd been here many times. He needed to get down to the basement level where the men's work clothes were, and he knew just how to do it.

It was still familiar territory to Benjamin when they stepped out through the sliding doors. Didn't look like anything had been changed much. He quickly found and selected nearly everything he wanted: a T-shirt, some boxer shorts, and a tan shirt.

The pants were more trouble. Looked like somebody had mixed them up; he couldn't seem to find his size. Well, they were bound to be here somewhere. He'd just have to keep looking.

"Can I help you?" The voice came from a dumpy, frizzy-haired woman, a clerk he vaguely remembered having seen before.

"Yes, I want a pair of 36-32 work pants. Can't seem to find them here where they usually are."

"Well, that's because we've moved them down to the other end of the counter." The woman moved briskly to the relocated pile and after a moment's search picked out a pair. "Here you are, sir."

She handed them over for his inspection, and Benjamin checked the size. Yes, they were just right.

"Fine," he said, handing them back.

"Anything else?"

"Uh—no, I believe this is everything."

"All right, sir—cash or charge?" the clerk asked, heading for the nearest cash register.

"Cash."

She took his proffered bill and turned toward the cash register. Then she hesitated and half-turned back, eyeing him quizzically for a moment.

"You know, somehow I feel like I should know you," she said. "Have we met before?"

"No, I don't think so. I've shopped in this store before. You probably remember me from that."

"Well—maybe." She made another abortive move toward the cash register but stopped again. "No, there's something else. I know! Didn't I see your picture in the paper awhile back? Why, you're that man—last name's Wright, isn't it—that man who disappeared from a nursing home!"

A spasm of fear caught and held him for a moment. He could do and say nothing. As he stood helplessly he saw Jon suddenly push between him and the sales clerk.

"No, he isn't!" Jon spouted loudly. "He isn't that man at all! He's my grandfather, that's who he is, and his name is— Irwin. Irwin, that's what it is, same as my mother's name before she got married. He doesn't even live here; he's just visiting us from California. He just got here yesterday, so he couldn't be that man you're talking about . . . "

Benjamin came to with a start as Jon's story ballooned. He

must get hold of things, mustn't let the boy keep babbling on like that.

"Jon!" he spoke firmly, and the boy halted his tirade to turn a questioning look to him. "Jon, you take that package and go over there by the elevator and wait for me."

"But—I don't want to go off, not while she's trying to say that you—"

"Jon." It was a dead serious order now. "Do as I say."

Then after a moment the boy, puzzled and hesitant still, hitched the bundle up under his arm and moved slowly in the bidden direction.

"Now then," Benjamin announced, turning back to the clerk, "I don't think it is necessary for you to know my life history in order to take my money and give me my change, is it?"

"Well, no—but—"

"Then I would like to have my change now, please."

The clerk turned to the cash register and hastily went about the routine of digging out the needed coins, dumping the purchases in a bag and stapling on the sales slip.

"Here you are, sir," she announced upon completing the process, "thank you and come again." But in spite of the assurance in the very ordinary phrases that she spoke, he saw that she watched him closely as he turned to go, and he knew he was not safe here. He must get away from this store as quickly as possible.

He walked unhurriedly to the elevator and waited there with Jon with seeming patience for the doors to open. But when they stepped out on the first floor level he picked up his pace, and after they had passed through the great glass doors at the front of the store he stretched his legs into the fastest walk his ancient frame could sustain.

"We'd better get a move on," he told Jon breathlessly. "That woman just may send somebody looking for me."

Jon didn't say anything, but he set his pace to match the old man's, and they hurried together to the nearest street corner. Then they turned to get quickly out of sight and walked to the middle of the block, where they left the sidewalk, crossed the street and turned into an alley. All the way through the next block they followed the alley, then crossed another street and plunged into a second. By the time they came to the end of that alley, Benjamin was craving more air than he could draw in at this pace, so he stopped and propped himself against the rough brick wall of an old building to rest. While he stood there, puffing and sweating, Jon peered out into the street in both directions.

"See anything?" Benjamin asked when he had caught his breath a little. "Any police cars—or anything?"

Jon shook his head and slouched back against the opposite wall, but he didn't say anything, and he didn't look at Benjamin either. He just stood and stared down at an idly scuffing foot.

"So," thought Benjamin to himself, "I must have hurt his feelings back there at the store. Better try to mend things if I can." He waited a moment to collect his thoughts, and then he spoke.

"Sorry if I came across a little too hard on you back there, Jon. I didn't mean to be so cranky, but I had to get you stopped."

Jon turned his eyes to his friend, but then he looked quickly away again. His mouth showed a tremor when he spoke.

"Well, why? Why did you want to stop me? I was just trying to get that lady not to think you were—who you are."

"I know. I know you were just trying to help. But, Jon, what you were saying wasn't true. I couldn't have you telling a big whopper like that."

"You mean that was the reason you stopped me?"

"Yes."

"But why?" Bewilderment came into the child's voice. "What difference did it make if it kept you out of trouble?"

"The difference is—it was a lie. I don't want you helping me by telling things that aren't true."

"But . . . " Still the boy didn't understand.

"Jon, it's wrong to lie."

With that the boy's questions were silenced. He understood, and yet he didn't understand. Hadn't anybody ever taught the boy anything? Benjamin wondered. He was a well-meaning youngster, but there were some big gaps in his knowledge of right and wrong. Maybe his folks had never gotten around to teaching him any simple everyday ethics. A child had to have some prodding to get halfway civilized. He could remember a few boyhood woodshed trips that had improved his own character considerably. And he in turn had had some sessions with his children, although he hadn't been one to rely so much on the woodshed. One way or another though, he'd gotten the message across. But it looked like nobody had bothered much with Jon. A pity, but the boy wasn't too old to learn. He had a whole lifetime ahead of him in which to learn, and he was the kind who would try, Benjamin could tell that.

"How far are we from a bus stop?" he asked the boy then, wanting to change to a more comfortable topic. "One that would take us back toward the park."

"There's one right at the end of this block," Jon answered, "but I don't know how long it'll be before a bus comes. They probably run pretty often along here though."

Benjamin pondered for a few moments. He didn't really want to leave the safety of the alley to go stand there exposed to view. Not this close to the store.

"Tell you what," he suggested. "Would you go down to the corner and watch for the bus? Then you could wave to me or something when you see it coming."

"All right."

With a bound the boy leaped out of the alley and went jogging down the sidewalk. When he had reached the corner he leaned casually against a lamp post and waited, watching faithfully for the first sign of an approaching bus. Five minutes passed. Then ten. Benjamin began to grow weary standing still so long, but he shifted his weight back and forth from one tired foot to the other and waited as patiently as he could.

Then at last Jon looked his way and gave a quick jerk of his hand to signal the approach of the bus. Benjamin stepped from the alley and hurried as fast as he could down the walk, arriving at the street corner in time to see the bus stopped a block away.

Soon they were on board and moving away from the area. Benjamin counted the blocks for a while, until they had passed ten. Then he quit bothering, for they were far away from the department store now, and he began to feel safer. If the clerk had called the police about him, he supposed they might be looking for him almost anywhere. On the other hand, he didn't know for sure whether he was still counted as a missing person or not. Perhaps after Janet got his letter she had stopped them from looking for him, but he doubted it. She wasn't one to give up on anything easily. Anyway, he had no way of knowing, and it was best to be careful. He wasn't going to go up to some policeman to ask directions, that's for sure!

He sat and thought about how strange it was to feel himself a fugitive from the law until a dig of Jon's elbow into his ribs startled him, and he turned to get the boy's whisper.

"This is about as close to the park as we can get on this bus. We'd better get off at the next stop."

Once on the curb again, Benjamin took a deep breath and gathered his strength for the long walk ahead. Then he set himself a steady pace and marched down the street as sturdily as he could. He managed to hold up until they reached the park, but then he had to rest, so he settled himself on a park bench and waited while Jon went for hot dogs and soda pop. They ate that and were still hungry, so he sent the boy back for seconds, then for candy bars. All this time he was so taken up with resting and eating that he forgot about being on the lookout for police or people who know him. He just didn't have the strength to bother about it any more. But his luck held. Nobody paid the least attention to the old man and the little boy who sat quietly on a park bench cramming down hot dogs.

When they at last finished eating, he found himself almost stranded. His legs didn't want to carry him any further. Jon helped pull him to his feet, and with the boy serving as a prop he tottered off across the park. When they reached the far side Benjamin gritted his teeth and plunged into the woods without stopping. He was afraid that the next time he stopped he wouldn't be able to get going again at all, so he forced himself on, leaning more and more on the boy for help in the difficult places.

At last they made it back to the camp. They stepped into the little clearing, and it was like coming home. Benjamin staggered to the lean-to and dropped onto his bed of leaves. He managed a feeble grin to Jon, but for a long while he didn't exert himself even to speak a single word.

Chapter 5

Benjamin stayed put at the campsite for a long time after that. It was better not to take such chances, he decided. Besides, he had everything he needed now. There was no reason to undertake another shopping expedition. He was quite content living quietly and simply in the woods. In fact, he could not remember a more blessed time since his childhood. For when, since then, had he had such a succession of golden days, strung together on the strand of a whole summer's length, to devote to nothing but resting on the warm bosom of a bit of untrammeled earth?

It could not last. Far back in his mind Benjamin knew that, but he kept the knowledge hidden away and seldom brought it out, for the summer stretched still a good way before him, and he would not ruin his contentment by anticipating the season's end.

The days were good for Jon too, it seemed. The lad was relaxing into the security of a trusted companionship.

The boy still kept something back from his friend, though, something he clutched to himself. The old man wondered about the moments of withdrawal, but he did not pry. A child deserved his privacy, same as anybody else. If the time came that Jon wanted to talk about whatever was bothering him, so be it. That time would have to come of its own; he would not rush it.

Finally it did come.

The day began like any other, soft and warm and quiet. Benjamin puttered around the fireside getting his breakfast, then slumped against a tree to await Jon's arrival. He glanced at the fishing poles resting against a nearby tree and rather hoped that

Jon wouldn't want to go fishing this morning. It was starting out to be a real hot day, and even the small effort it would take to follow the path to the nearest fishing hole seemed too much. Besides, the stream was shrinking with the dry weather, and the fish weren't biting very well. Still, if the boy had his heart set on it he'd go along. In the meantime, until Jon came, he'd just relax.

He leaned his head back against the tree and surrendered to the lethargy that gradually came over him. He dozed for a while, then roused to get a book that Jon had brought him and sauntered down to the stream where he settled himself onto a mossy spot to read. That way he could either listen to the book or to the muted murmurings of the stream, and he did both. After a while he dozed again. Thus the morning passed, and still Jon did not come.

He was surprised, for Jon had been showing up fairly early every morning. Well, something had probably come up. He'd go ahead and fix himself a sandwich for lunch with the peanut butter and jelly he had on hand, for it looked like Jon wasn't going to get here in time with any fresh groceries.

He ate the small meal without much relish, for he had grown accustomed to the boy's company at mealtimes, and eating by himself wasn't much fun.

He sat on the log and waited, turning at the slightest sound to the direction from which he thought Jon would come. He wasn't sleepy now. Yet, somehow, when he tried to read further in the book he made little progress. His eyes passed over the words, but his mind would not take them in. He gave up after a while and laid the book aside. Benjamin could only think about Jon and wonder why he had not come. He felt a growing uneasiness about the boy, and yet he chided himself for worrying when he had no real reason to do so. A dozen things could have come up to keep him away. It was silly to fret. Yet despite his reasonings he could not shake the feeling that something was wrong.

At last he could sit still no longer. He got up from the log and prowled aimlessly about the camp. Then he strolled down the path, drawn by a desire to meet the boy a bit sooner should he be coming along that way. All was silent this hot, still afternoon. No twig cracked with an approaching footstep, no leaf rustled from a brushing hand. It grew more lonely in the woods, for the quiet only enhanced his sense of solitude, so after a while he turned his steps back to the campsite. There he waited.

At last, he gave up hope. Sundown came and twilight began to gather, and the boy had not come. Now he could not be expected until tomorrow.

Benjamin tried to shed his feeling of disappointment and worry by busying himself about the campfire, stirring it and adding fresh wood, setting a pan of water to heat for coffee, then making a couple of pieces of toast. It was all the supper he wanted. When his small meal was eaten, he sat and stared awhile at the glowing coals which shone ever more brightly as the darkness pressed closer around. He decided it might as well be bedtime, so he put a couple of long-lasting chunks of wood on the fire and turned to the lean-to. He had almost let himself down onto the bed when he heard something, or at least thought he did. Was it a tiny, distant splash? He hesitated, wondering. Then—yes, he did hear footsteps, and they were drawing close, almost here! He turned eagerly toward the spot where the trail entered the campsite, and, sure enough, out stepped Jon.

"Well, now!" he gave hearty greeting. "I'd about given up on you."

Jon didn't say anything. He turned a blank face to Benjamin for a few seconds, then went to the log and sat down. Strange behavior, Benjamin thought. He hadn't even said hello.

"What happened? Get held up somehow or other today?"

Still there was no answer. The boy sat silent, scarcely seeming to have heard. Benjamin started around the end of the log to draw nearer to him. When he did so, he saw the back of Jon's head, and halted in his tracks. There clotted in a tangled mass of hair was blood. Quite a bit of blood. Why, the boy had been hurt, and it didn't look like the wound had been tended at all!

"Jon, what happened? Looks like you've gotten a pretty bad cut on your head. It's been bleeding quite a bit." He leaned down to examine the wound, but it was too dark to see much. "Here, turn around with your back to the fire so I can have a look."

For a few seconds Jon remained motionless, but then he slowly maneuvered himself around. Benjamin still couldn't see how bad the wound was, for too much dark, clotted blood covered the spot. At least he knew that it needed to be cleaned and treated.

"Jon, you know I'm always glad to have you around here. But I really think you'd better hustle on home right now and get this taken care of. How in the world did it happen anyway?"

"I just—backed into something." A few muttered words came out of the boy at last, but Benjamin knew they were not true. Jon had not gotten such an injury by backing into something.

"Well, anyway—however it happened—you'd better go let your mother tend to it."

"No!" Jon spit out the word vehemently, and Benjamin was surprised, for it was the first time the boy had ever refused to do what he'd asked.

"Why, Jon? Why not?"

"I'm not going home tonight. I'm going to stay here."

For a moment Benjamin was speechless. Whatever had gotten into the boy? He'd never acted this way before. Maybe his family situation wasn't the best in the world, but he'd always been willing to go home before. Something must have really gone wrong.

"But Jon," he argued, "you can't stay here all night. You know that. Your folks will be worried half to death about you."

The boy turned a strange look to him, and then his lips parted into a smile that wasn't really a smile at all.

"No, they won't," he said. "They won't worry at all. Dad's not even home."

"Well, what about your mother? She'd worry. You must go on home, Jon."

The boy rose to his feet and stared at Benjamin for a long moment. Benjamin returned the look, and his eyes gave out a determination that remained firm.

"Okay." The boy turned from him. "If you won't let me stay here, I'll leave. But I'm not going home."

"Now, Jon, you mustn't be that way." Benjamin reached for

the boy and grasped his arm. "If you've had a fuss with your mother—whatever has happened—you can't do her like that. Think how she'd feel if she knew you were hurt."

"If she knew I was hurt?" The boy turned wild eyes to him again, and his boyish treble broke into a strange laugh that shrilled almost to a scream. "If she knew I was hurt?" Then the dam broke, and the tightly-held truth spewed out at last. "She's the one who did it!"

For a moment Benjamin stood amazed. What was the boy saying? That his mother had delivered the injury? But how? Was it an accident? Or something else, something so appalling he could barely think of it.

Then he found his voice and tried to halt the boy's dreadful laughter. "Jon! Jon, listen to me!"

But the cries that were not mirth but rather a mockery of it kept on coming.

"Jon! Stop it!" He grabbed the child by both arms and held him firmly so he could look squarely into his eyes. Still the laughter came. In desperation, Benjamin shook the boy, one hard shake, and then another. Finally the sounds ceased, choked back into the thin, contorted throat.

"Now, Jon," Benjamin let the words out carefully. "I must find out about this. I must know exactly what has happened. Do you understand? I want to know the whole truth."

The boy stared silently back at him, then nodded his head.

"Now, what were you saying about your mother—hurting you? Was it an accident?"

The child's lips quivered once, but then they parted, and the one word that came out was calmly spoken.

"No."

"Then—are you saying she did it on purpose?"

"Yes." There was no hesitation in the answer.

"How did she—did she hit you with something?"

"A spatula."

"A spatula?"

"Yes, you know. One of those things you turn eggs with."

"Oh—yes. Well, why did she do it?"

"Well, she was kind of mad at me this morning. I woke her

up too early for one thing. She sleeps late, and I knocked a bottle off a shelf in the bathroom. It made a big noise, and she woke up. Then I was in the kitchen, and I fried an egg for breakfast. She came in, but I didn't see she was right behind me, and I picked up my plate with the egg on it and turned around and bumped into her. The egg was real greasy, and it slid off the plate onto her robe and made a big spot on it. Then it fell on down onto the floor and made a mess. That's when she got real mad at me." He glanced uneasily at Benjamin as if wondering whether he too would find the offense worthy of a blow. "But I didn't mean to do it! It was an accident."

"You mean she hit you on the head for spilling the egg?" Benjamin asked.

"Yes."

"Is that all there was to it, just spilling the egg?"

"Yes."

A sickness wrenched Benjamin's middle as the import of the boy's story reached him. He had guessed that things were not all they should be in Jon's home, but he hadn't suspected anything like this. How could it be? A mother injuring her own son like that! It was beyond the realm of his understanding. Such things just did not happen in his world. Yet he remembered reading in the newspaper about cases of child abuse, so he guessed there really were people who committed such crimes. Suddenly he recalled other things, the black eye, the sore elbow, the cut lip.

"Jon, what about those other times you were hurt? The black eye and your cut lip? And the sore arm? Was it—your mother?" Even now he could hardly come right out and say the words.

Mutely the boy nodded. Again a wave of horror swept through Benjamin. To think that this had been happening to this boy, this child who had so generously befriended him.

"Do you think—" Jon started to ask, but he seemed not to know how to put his question.

"Yes?" Benjamin suddenly became aware of a hint of cringing in the boy's manner.

"Well, do you think it was—right for my mother to—"

"To punish you like that?" Why, the boy didn't really know

what he thought about it! Perhaps he thought all parents treated their children that way. "No!" the word exploded from him. "It wasn't right, Jon. There isn't anything in this world that a child could ever do that would deserve punishment like that!"

The boy's eyes filled with tears that began sliding down his cheeks, and Benjamin gathered him in his arms and held him tight. Once before he had held this child as he wept, but then he hadn't known the reason for the tears.

Now he knew, and the knowledge brought a few tears of his own which dropped on the tousled head pressed hard against Benjamin's breast. The closeness stirred memories of comforting small boys many years ago, and without really intending to, Benjamin found himself humming a familiar and comforting tune, one he and Kate had sung countless times to comfort their own young ones. In a quavering voice, he sang the lyrics as he held Jon tightly against his body.

"What a friend we have in Jesus, all our sins and griefs to bear.

"What a privilege to carry, everything to God in prayer."

He paused for a moment, catching his breath. Jon was motionless, leaning against him.

"Have we trials and temptations, is there trouble anywhere?

"We should never be discouraged, take it to the Lord in prayer."

Then they sat silently for a long time, watching the flickering light of the campfire. Finally, the tears were gone and the boy seemed calmer.

Suddenly, Jon stirred and moved a bit away from the safety of his friend's encircling arms. He had another question to ask.

"What about tonight?" A touch of belligerence had returned to his voice. "I won't go back home!"

"No," Benjamin agreed with a sigh. "No, you can't go back home. You must stay here with me tonight."

Satisfied at last, Jon went happily to the lean-to and began arranging the blanket over the bed of leaves. Meanwhile Benjamin set a pan of water over the fire to heat and began to tend to Jon's wound.

To think that the boy's own mother had dealt such a blow!

Anger rose up within Benjamin again until his fingers trembled as he finished up the job and wrapped a clean undershirt around the boy's head.

Jon stretched out in the lean-to, and fell asleep quickly, but drowsiness did not come quickly to Benjamin. His thoughts about the events of the day turned into pricks of worry that would not let his mind rest. There had been nothing to do but keep the boy here with him tonight surely, and they were probably safe for now, but what about tomorrow? He would have to do something about Jon, but what? He couldn't turn to the authorities for help, for then he himself would be caught. He couldn't send the boy back home—not to that home. Besides, it was obvious that Jon had reached some kind of breaking point and wouldn't go back home. He couldn't turn the youngster loose to fend for himself. Jon was resourceful, but he was hardly ready to be on his own yet. Benjamin would have to do something, but what?

They'd talk it over first thing in the morning. Maybe Jon had some relatives who would take him in and work things out. He hoped so.

Benjamin loved the boy, but he was an old man having enough trouble looking after himself. How could he look after a child? Still, they had gotten on well together, and he hated to think of their being separated. One did not break apart such a friendship lightly. Maybe somehow they could manage to stick together, but just now he didn't see how. The worrisome thoughts continued to whirl themselves about in his head until, totally wearied by them, he dropped off into a brief, troubled sleep.

Morning came at last after the long, restless night, but he was not particularly glad to see it. He kept his eyes closed at first against the probing sunbeams that slanted down into the lean-to. Sounds of softened footsteps and snapping kindling told him that Jon was up and stirring about, so he guessed he'd better wake up and face the day.

Gingerly he pried himself up from his bed, moving slowly as usual until he got his joints limbered up. Then he joined Jon at the fireside, and they went quietly and companionably about getting their breakfast. When they had eaten they sat silently side by side on the log while Benjamin drank a second cup of coffee and tried to get his thoughts together.

"Jon," he asked at last, "do you have any relatives? Besides your folks, I mean?"

"No, not around here."

"You mean you do have some living in other places?"

"Yes."

"Well, where are they?"

"Oh, a long way off. Dad's mother is dead, but his father is alive. He lives back east somewhere—Pittsburgh, I think it is. Mom's mother lives in Canada some place. I've never seen her. She's divorced. I don't think Mom knows where her father is."

"Have you got any aunts or uncles?"

"Uhmm—I think only one. Dad has a sister. But I don't know where she lives."

"Do you know her name?"

"Her first name's Julia."

"What about her last name?"

"I can't seem to think of it. She's married, so it would be different from Dad's. She and her husband came to see us once when I was real little, but I can't remember what their name was."

It didn't look like there was going to be any help close at hand from Jon's family.

"Is there anybody at all living around here—not relatives, just friends—who could look after you? People you could—trust?"

Jon turned sober, questioning eyes on him. "Why, there's you," he said.

"Yes," Benjamin responded, turning away for a moment from the open face before him. "Yes, there's me. But I'm an old man, Jon, too old to be looking after a boy your age. You need someone younger. Isn't there anybody else you could go to?"

"No."

"Just think now, there must be someone."

"No, there isn't! There isn't anybody but you."

Benjamin sat silent for a long minute as he felt the burden

settling firmly about his shoulders. Then he heard the boy's soft voice.

"But if you don't want me hanging around with you I won't," he said. Then his voice rose to a shriller tone. "I can get along by myself anyway! I don't need to have anybody looking after me!"

"Now, Jon," Benjamin protested, "you know it isn't that I don't want you with me!" He paused and studied the look of doubt that had sprung up in the boy's eyes. "You're a good friend, and I like to have you around. You've been a lot of help to me too. I don't know how I would have gotten along without you. I don't know how I would get along without you now. But what I'm getting at is—you need somebody better than me to look after you and—help work things out for you."

The boy answered him only with a silent stare.

"All right," Benjamin said with a sigh. "We won't bother any more about it right now." He knew he was failing to come up with any answers, but he didn't know what to do. He got up and began to putter about with the clean-up chores, rinsing out the coffee pot and pouring the grounds into a garbage pit they'd dug.

"We're getting pretty short on groceries," Benjamin announced. "Better get some shopping done today."

"Yes," Jon agreed after a moment's hesitation, "but I don't know if it's safe for me to go to the store. Do you think they might be looking for me? Like they did for you when you first left that place you were staying?"

Of course. It was not only possible but likely. Suddenly a frightening thought struck Benjamin.

"Jon," he asked, "does your mother know that you spend a lot of time here at the park? Do you think she might send the police here looking for you?"

"Well, she does know I come here a lot. She might tell them. Yes, she probably would!"

"Then, we aren't safe here any more! They might not search way back here in the woods right away, but I bet they will get around to it sooner or later." The old fear surged in him again, fear not only for Jon but for himself. If Jon were caught, he would be caught too. "Jon, I'm afraid we're going to have to leave this place!"

"Well, okay," Jon agreed, "but where can we go? I don't know any more good hiding places!"

"I don't either! Not here in town." The fear rose up now to clutch at his throat. It seemed there was no place for them to go. Oh, if only he were home! Back on his farm with the hills and woods all around, country that he knew like the back of his hand. There were plenty of places there where they could stay out of sight, places where nobody would ever find them. If only they were there instead of here in the city, they'd be all right. He'd know what to do there, how to get along. He always had.

Suddenly he was determined. That was what they would do. They'd go home! They'd have to get away from here, slip through the net he felt drawing about them. They could do it if they were careful. They'd travel at night when nobody would be likely to recognize them and go by the back roads that were little used during the late hours. He knew well all the possible routes between the city and his farm. It wouldn't be hard to find his way. Besides the roads, he knew short cuts they could take across neighboring farms.

The farm was a long way. His enthusiasm faltered a bit at the thought. It was 21 miles from the city limits to his home by the main road and more than that by the back roads. Probably 24—maybe 25 miles. But they could do it. Surely they could. They could walk a few miles every night. Three, maybe four or five if he were up to it.

He wished he were stronger. A couple of years ago he could have managed a hike like that with no trouble at all. Now though—well, he still thought he could do it. He'd take it easy and try not to overtax himself. After all, there was no deadline set for their arrival. They could take as long as necessary for the trip. Just a few miles at a time would get them there eventually.

He turned to the boy to talk it over, and a vigor born of hope and enthusiasm brightened his voice.

"Jon, how would you like to go with me out to my farm for a while?"

"You mean way out in the country where you used to live?"

"Yes."

"Sure that'd be fine with me. You think that's a safe place to be?"

"Yes. At least the safest place I know."

"But don't some other people have your farm now?"

"Now, they don't own it. They're just renting, and they only use the house and garden plot and a pasture for their cow. I still own it all, and we can certainly stay on any of my land that they aren't using."

"That sounds like a good idea to me. Boy, I bet nobody would ever think of looking for me way out there!" Jon paused and thought a moment. "But how are we going to get there?"

"Well, I guess we'll have to walk. We can't very well hitch a ride. Somebody might recognize us. I think it would be best to travel at night and stay holed up somewhere during the daytime. Do you think we can walk all that way? It's about 25 miles by the route I want to take."

"Sure! I like to hike, I know I can do it—if you . . . " Jon turned a questioning look to Benjamin, but he didn't come right out and ask.

"Oh, I think I can make it all right," Benjamin said, reassuring both Jon and himself. "We'll take it easy and not try to go too far at a time. It'll take several days."

"Well, when do we start?"

"We'd better leave tonight, I think. In fact, I'm a little nervous about staying here the rest of the day. Let's figure out what we want to take with us."

It was hard to leave anything behind, for their equipment was meager to start with. Most of their cooking utensils went into a pile to take along, and added to that was the supply of groceries. Jon had bought plenty several days earlier. They wouldn't try to take their fishing poles, but they certainly wanted the gear, so they cut the line loose and carefully wound it around a short stick to keep it from tangling until they were ready to use it again. They would need it, for fishing had always been good in the little creek that ran across his place, and he was sure they'd be wanting to wet their lines as soon as they got there. They'd probably be needing the fish to eat by then!

In less than an hour, they were ready to go. They had even stripped the plastic cover from the lean-to in case it rained on them enroute.

The rest of the day Benjamin tried to relax and gather his strength as much as he could. It wasn't easy to relax totally when he knew searchers might come poking through the brush any time, and an hour before dusk he was up and ready to go. They could travel to the edge of the park while it was still light.

Hoisting their packs to their shoulders, they took one last look at the campsite that had been a happy home to them and started out. In minutes they were at the clearing, ready to emerge for the last time from their wilderness. Benjamin was thinking that it wouldn't hurt if they stopped once more at the refreshment stand, so they could start on full stomachs.

Suddenly there was a tug at his shirt-tail and he heard Jon's hoarse whisper, "Stop! Stop! Don't you see them?"

"Who?"

"The police?"

"No! Where?"

"Right over there—see, their car's parked beside the refreshment stand."

Benjamin peered out through the trees. Yes, there sat a blue and white car in plain view. And standing at the refreshment stand were two uniformed figures.

"Well," he said softly, trying to judge their intent from their stance, "it could be that they just stopped to get something to eat."

"Yes, but we don't know for sure. They might be looking for me!"

Just then the two officers turned and began peering about the park. To Benjamin and Jon it seemed the men were looking right at them.

"We'd better go some other way," Jon said, fear again reducing his voice to a whisper.

They drew back into the woods a little to be sure they were out of sight. "I know a good way out of here," said Jon. "Just follow me."

Pacing himself carefully so the old man could keep up, Jon

led the way down a trail Benjamin had never seen before until they emerged once again on the banks of the little creek. Then Jon followed it downstream until, in a short time, they reached a spot where the stream led out of the park and under a big culvert that passed beneath a quiet stretch of suburban road.

"What do we do now?" asked Jon.

"Well, let me think—what road is this, do you know? Is it Brenner Road?"

"Yes, that's the name of it."

"I thought so." Benjamin nodded his head with satisfaction. "I know right where we are then. This road will do fine as a starting place. We'll go a couple of miles farther out from town on this road and then turn east for a ways." He took a few steps across a shallow ditch and moved up to the edge of the asphalt strip, peering in both directions for cars. None were in sight now, but there would be. This was a fairly well traveled road, for people had been moving out to the suburban areas it served.

"We'd better find a bit of cover somewhere and wait a while," he told Jon. "I can't be diving for the ditch every time a car comes along."

"Well, why don't we cross over to the other side. See, there's a clump of trees over there. Maybe we could get out of sight and wait there."

"Okay, let's try it."

With one more quick look to be sure no cars were coming, Benjamin hurried across the road with Jon scuttling along behind. Gratefully they slipped into a secluded spot and settled themselves on the grassy sod. There, Benjamin lay back and rested and thought. How strange a predicament he and the boy found themselves in. They were both fugitives from the law when you came right down to it. It seemed incredible to him, for there'd never been a more law-abiding citizen than he was! He wasn't sure what the law had to do with keeping him in that nursing home, but he supposed that if his kids thought he had to stay there the law would go along with it. If that were the case, he guessed he'd have to admit to being a lawbreaker. Then there was Jon; what about him? Goodness knows the boy hadn't done anything wrong, but he supposed that his folks would have the law out looking for him. Yes, it was all very strange to think about. He didn't really understand. Too many confusing things were happening.

Well, he didn't need to understand but one thing now—he was going home. That was all he needed to know. A few days of journeying and he'd be back to his own place where he knew every tree, every rock, almost every blade of grass. Surely all would come right there. Things would work out somehow. All he had to worry about was getting there.

"Lord, help me to get back home," he prayed silently as he stretched himself out on the bed of grass and drifted into a fitful doze. "Please help me—and Jon too—to get back home . . ."

Chapter 6

They waited and rested in their hideaway until the vehicle traffic subsided almost to nothing. They said little to each other as they nestled in the haven of the tiny wood, for each was numbed by the events that had swept so quickly upon them, and each was also a little fearful of what might be ahead. They had grown secure and comfortable in their little camp in the park, and now it was painful to be driven from that sanctuary. But the farm would be even better than the park, Benjamin reminded himself. If they could just get there.

"Do you think we ought to eat something?" Jon's voice came quavering at last out of the nearby darkness.

"Yes, I suppose we should. I'm not really very hungry though."

"No, me neither."

He could hear Jon rummaging in the grocery bag, and he crept over to join the boy beneath a sheltering shrub.

"Can't hardly see what I'm doing," Jon murmured. "Here's the bread though. What do you want?"

"Oh, just give me a piece of bread and some raisins to start with."

Bread and raisins was all they had for their late supper. Each managed, against a lack of appetite, to swallow that much, and then they were thirsty and drank from the stream to finish their meal.

By now it seemed a long time since a pair of headlights had brightened the treetops over their heads or a truck's roar had drowned their voices.

"Think it's safe to start out now?" Jon asked, moving restlessly about the little grove.

"Yes, I reckon we'd better get going." Benjamin bent his stiff joints and with a muffled groan began pulling himself to his feet.

Jon gathered up the bag of groceries in one arm and their blanketed bundle in the other.

"Wait a minute while I take this stuff on up, and then I'll come back and lend you a hand."

"All right," Benjamin agreed reluctantly, for he hated having to be helped like that. It was a wonder the boy didn't get tired of it. But he knew he probably would need aid to get back up onto the road in the dark, and he'd best just wait here until he got it.

Once under way, the anticipation of seeing his home place spurred Benjamin's footsteps into a quicker pace, and for a while they moved briskly down the road. It was a dark night, unusually cloud overhead for this time of the summer. But they could see well enough to make their way along the smooth strip of asphalt without difficulty, and they made good time. It was surprising how soon they covered the two miles to where they turned off this road and headed east on Merritsville Road.

"Are we going through Merrittsville?" Jon asked when he spied the sign.

"No, no. That's a good ten miles on down the line, and we're going to turn south again long before there. Are you getting tired?" he asked, noting Jon shifting the grocery bag in his arms.

"Well—not much."

"Maybe we'd better rest a few minutes before we go on."

"Okay."

Benjamin laid his burden down and leaned gratefully against the signpost while Jon sprawled on the road's shoulder.

"How far have we come?" the boy asked after a moment.

"It's about two miles from the edge of town to this corner," Benjamin answered.

"We're pretty far out in the country already then, aren't we?" Jon asked, heaving a sigh of satisfaction.

Benjamin smiled. He guessed two miles out of town did seem like a long way to a city child.

"Yes, we've come quite a ways," he agreed, "but we've still got a long, long way to go."

"Maybe we'd better get started again then, huh?"

"Oh—I think maybe we need to rest a few minutes longer. At least I do." Now that he'd stopped, Benjamin could feel a quivering in his legs, so he held to the post and with a grunt let himself down onto the ground, then leaned back, using the post as a back rest. It was sure good to get off his feet for a while. But actually he was holding up very well. They should be able to get in at least another couple of miles before they had to stop. Let's see, that would bring them about to the old Hanson place. Nobody lived there any more. In fact, the house had been torn down, but there was a good barn still standing beside the road. If nobody were around, that might be a good place to spend the day.

"We'd better get going," he said. "Daylight comes early this time of year."

The two trudged on down the road through the wee, dark hours. They had to stop to rest again after half an hour, and once more after that, and it was harder each time for Benjamin to get up and start walking. He did though, and finally they arrived safely at the intersection where they were to head south again.

"There, see that barn?" Benjamin asked, pointing out a large, leaning structure off to the left as they turned onto the narrow gravel road. It stood silhouetted against the barely lightening eastern sky, and Benjamin noticed that it was not in as good condition as he had remembered. It had a decided list to the west. However, it would serve their purposes well enough. All they needed was a secluded spot where nobody would notice them and some shelter from the heat of the midday sun. The barn would furnish that.

They turned their footsteps onto a heavily weeded but still discernible driveway and walked past a sagging gate into a long deserted front yard. A faint scent of roses wafted on the night air to meet them, and Benjamin could make out the shaggy shapes of several sprawling shrubs nearby. Looked like some of Martha Hanson's rose bushes were still growing, and they had a few blooms on them even this late in the summer!

Strange to think that the roses had so long survived the one who had planted them. He hadn't thought about Martha or her husband Tom for a long time. They were good people. Seemed sad that their home place, once well cared for and full of life, was now deserted, but that's the way it went. The old folks were long gone, and none of the kids had wanted to stay on the place.

The house had partially burned, he remembered, when some careless renters who didn't know how to use a wood stove had started a fire. What was left of it had been torn down for scrap lumber and hauled away. Then the farm itself had been divided into two parcels and sold to neighbors who had it all in pasture now. At least the barn still stood though. He turned and walked across what was once the barn lot to the dark cavern of the barn's doorway.

"Sure is gloomy in here," Jon commented uneasily as they stepped inside.

"Yep. It'll lighten up when the sun comes up. Probably nothing in here to bother us, except cobwebs maybe." He swept his hand before his face to ward off one that he had already encountered. "Tell you what, why don't we put our stuff down here inside the door and then go look for water before it gets too light?"

"Okay. I sure am thirsty."

"Yes, me too. We'll need something to dip it in."

They set their burdens down, and Jon began rummaging around in the bundle of cooking gear.

"How about the coffee pot?" he asked.

"That ought to do fine. Now, right directly east of the house—well, let's go back outside where we can see." They stepped back out into the barn lot and turned in the direction Benjamin pointed. "Now, look right off up there where that little rise is—do you see it? Just the other side of that is a shallow gully, and down in the gully there is a nice little spring. At least there used to be."

"Want me to go look for it?"

"Yes. If you don't mind going by yourself, I think I'll just wait here."

"Sure."

With a quick duck under a fence, Jon went bounding off into the pasture, waving the coffee pot wildly as he leaped and dashed along his way.

Moments later he was back. "There wasn't much water there," he said, "but I managed to dip up a half a pot. Here, you go ahead and drink all this. I had a drink while I was at the spring." He handed Benjamin the coffee pot and offered an apology as the old man tipped it up. "It might be a little bit muddy. I couldn't keep all the dirt out."

He was right, it did taste muddy, but Benjamin was too thirsty to care.

They knelt in the barn doorway then and began pulling things out of the grocery bag, for both were hungry now after their long walk.

"How about some dried beef?" Benjamin asked, holding up a small jar.

"Sounds good."

"I feel better now," Jon announced, after they had eaten the dried beef sandwiches, some raisins, and a couple of candy bars.

"Yes, me too. Well, no wonder—we didn't eat much last night for supper."

They sat quietly then, one against each door jamb, and watched the morning come. They could almost feel the early light pushing past them into the gray gloom that sitll clung to the western hills and valleys. Already the air grew warm and a little sticky.

"Gonna be a scorcher today," Benjamin murmured.

"Uh-huh. I'm glad we don't have to be out in it. We are going to stay here all day, aren't we?"

"Yes, I think we'd better keep out of sight until well after dark again."

"Hey, I think I hear a car coming!"

They perked up their ears to listen, and, sure enough, a distant motor hum came to them. Then they saw a little dust cloud on the road to the south, and they knew the morning traffic had begun.

"Well," Benjamin grunted, heaving himself up onto his

knees, "I guess we'd better move inside."

Quickly they grabbed up the groceries that were strewn about the barn door and pulled them back out of sight. It was light enough inside the barn to see now, and Jon peered curiously about, cringing a bit from the touch of a great festoon of cobwebs that draped the wall beside him.

"Ever been in a barn before?" Benjamin asked.

"No, I never have."

"Well, this one's getting pretty old and dilapidated. Hasn't been used much for a long time. But you can still tell how things worked. See the stalls over there, and the stanchions that held the cows when they were being milked? See that ladder going up through the hole in the ceiling? That leads to the hayloft. Up there in the north end of the loft there's another door, the one they lifted the hay up through when they stored it."

"Can I climb up there and look around?"

"Sure." Benjamin smiled with his answer, for he'd been expecting the question. Boys always had an affinity for haylofts, even when there was no hay in them. "Just be a little careful. The boards might be loose or rotten somewhere."

That was all Jon needed to send him clambering hand over hand up the old ladder. Benjamin watched each step the boy took with a critical eye, then settled back with a satisfied nod. The ladder looked rickety, but it still held firm. Tom Hanson hadn't been a fancy builder, but he's been one to put things together so they'd stay. This whole barn, tipsy as it seemed, would probably stand here a good while longer yet before it gave way. Again it seemed strange to him that the works of a man's hands should so long outlast the man himself. For the man was the builder—the planter—the maker. In a sense, sometimes the creator. Yet Tom was long gone, while his barn remained. And Martha Hanson too lay still and silent beneath the sod up there in the old Oak Ridge cemetery, while each spring the plantings of her fingers drew from the same kind of earth that covered her, the stuff that made them spring to new life and thrust fresh growth up toward the sun. Too bad the earth could not so regenerate the fallen human bodies that lay tucked beneath its skin.

But why should he indulge such thoughts? Benjamin believed deep in his soul that this would be. Not a regeneration worked by the earth, of course, but by God, the Creator of both earth and man. Wasn't this the ancient doctrine? "In the twinkling of an eye. . . . " Yes, that was the promise. That's how it would be. For Tom and Martha Hanson. And for dear Kate, gone seven years now. And for him too. They would not be left to the works of rot and decay. He was comforted with the thought.

Then a call from above interrupted his ruminations.

"Hey, I found it!"

He'd almost forgotten about the boy, but now he looked up to see Jon's face peering at him from the big, square opening that gave the ladder entryway into the loft.

"What did you find?" he called back.

"That door you told me about. It's just like a big window with shutters on it. Except there isn't any glass in the window, and the bottom of it comes right down to the floor. The shutters work too. I got them open, and you can see a long way from up here."

"Yes, well, just see that you don't lean out too far. We don't want you falling and breaking an arm or something."

"Oh, I won't." And with that reassurance the face disappeared from view, and pattering footsteps indicated the boy was exploring the other end of the loft.

Benjamin smiled and wondered just what was the great attraction that a barn loft held for a child. He'd felt it as a boy, had loved poking about the great loft in his father's barn. His own children had been the same way, chasing each other up and down the ladder, romping over the stacks of baled hay. How often he's found Steven up there, curled up on a bale of hay with a book. A great bookworm that boy had been, and he'd loved reading in the loft on a rainy day when the rain drummed a quieting song on the metal roof. Yes, kids did have an affinity for barn lofts. And to think that Jon had never been in one before! This one was a poor excuse as a playground now, for there weren't any hay bales to climb over and build tunnels in, but he seemed to be having fun anyway.

As for Benjamin, he was beginning to feel a great weariness, a need for sleep that was strong enough to push aside all worries and concerns of yesterday and all plans for tomorrow. He must get some rest. Pulling the blanket after him, he crept back from the doorway to a spot that would be shaded all through the day and spread it out to make his bed. He wished for a pile of hay to cushion his rude pallet, but there was nothing but a stray wisp here and there. Not even enough to rake up for a pillow. So he folded his jacket to place beneath his head and stretched out on half the blanket, leaving space for Jon to join him. The boy would probably grow tired of knocking around up there in the loft after a while and would need to get some rest too. In the meantime, he was too sleepy to wait.

A half hour later, Jon realized that he was getting tired, curled up on the remaining edge of the blanket, and almost instantly dropped off into a dead-tired slumber. There they lay, the old man and the young one, sleeping away the gradually warming hours of the summer day.

It was the increasing heat of the afternoon that roused them. Benjamin woke first, feeling dry in the mouth but moist and sticky over all the rest of his body. He stirred from the blanket and moved toward the door hoping to find a cooling breeze there, but the air that drifted languidly through the doorway was even warmer than the stagnant air within. He moved back again and sat down against a post, fanning himself now and then with a flattened paper bag. He reached for the coffee pot, but it held barely an inch of lukewarm water in the bottom. He thought he'd left more than that. There was hardly a good swallow for each of them. He hesitated to take even that now, for Jon might need it even worse when he woke up. He painfully put the pot aside and waited.

It took another hour for Jon to get his sleep out, but he stirred at last and sat up on the blanket.

"Phew! Sure is hot," he said, wiping his damp forehead and pushing back a mop of unruly hair.

"Yes. Pretty warm all right."

"Is there anything left to drink?" Jon asked, eyeing the coffee pot.

"A little. Help yourself."

Jon picked up the pot, then he too hestitated when he saw how shallow was the disk of water glistening in the bottom.

"Have you had any?" he asked.

"Yes."

"I mean since this morning."

"Well, no. But I'm not very thirsty."

Jon turned to him with a long look, then spoke with the corners of his mouth tucking into the hint of a smile.

"I don't think you're telling me the truth," he said.

Benjamin gave back a look of astonishment. It was true; the boy had caught him in a lie. A self-sacrificing lie, but a lie all the same. And he'd been the one to make such a fuss about always telling the truth! He let out a chuckle which quickly grew into a laugh.

"I guess you're right," he said. "I guess I am a little bit— well, more than a little bit thirsty."

He accepted the pot then from Jon's outstretched hand and took two small swallows, about what he judged to be his share, then handed it back to Jon to finish. Then they both sat silently for a few minutes, thinking about their thirst.

"Do you think it would be safe for me to go back up to the spring real quick and get some more?" Jon asked at last.

"I don't know." Benjamin shook his head dubiously. "Let's see how much traffic there is."

They moved over near the door and watched, and in the next few minutes several cars swished by trailing great dust clouds that sifted down through the shimmering air to settle on the already heavily powdered roadside shrubbery.

"They're coming pretty often," Jon murmured at last.

"Yes. And I'm afraid that most anybody using this road would wonder if they saw somebody roaming about the place. Everybody knows that this farm has been deserted for a long time."

"Well, maybe we'd just better wait until it gets dark." Jon sighed as he gave up on the idea.

"Yes, I expect so. I should have sent you back to refill that pot early this morning. Then we would have had more water right here with us." Benjamin faulted himself for not having had that much foresight. He'd known they were going to be pretty much trapped in here all day; he should have realized they'd need more water. Oh, well, it couldn't be helped now, and they'd survive. They'd just have to tough it out for a few more hours until evening.

They moved back then from the hot air at the doorway to the slightly less torrid atmosphere of the interior to continue their wait. Benjamin stretched out on the blanket again and managed to doze intermittently, but Jon wandered restlessly about, then climbed into the loft again. It was too hot for comfort up there, so he didn't stay long. Finally he too sat down and waited.

At last the sun set, and the evening air came with a hint of cooling in it. More alert now, Benjamin could hardly wait until the treadmill of the long, long road had passed beneath his feet and he could step out onto his own sod once more. His mind's eye saw just where he'd leave the traveled way, strike off across the Erickson pasture, climb a grass-carpeted hill and step out onto the ridge that overlooked almost his whole farm. It was a glorious picture that came to him, lifting his spirit and refreshing his weary frame. All would be well when he got home. Yes, all would be well.

"Do you think it's dark enough to get water now?" Jon's voice startled him back to the present, and he turned to see the boy standing with the coffee pot in his hand.

"Well, let's see." He got up and stood in the doorway gauging the thickness of the gloom. The occasional passing car had its lights on now, and surely no one would notice a small boy moving about this far back from the road. Still he was cautious. "Be sure no cars are near when you start out," he instructed.

"Okay," Jon said. Moments later he was gone and had soon returned.

"Here you go," he said as he reached the old man's side and handed over an almost full container.

Benjamin drank deeply and satisfyingly, then took the tin away from his lips and turned to the boy.

"How about you?" he asked.

"I got a drink at the spring again, same as before. You can have all this."

Benjamin thankfully lifted the pot to his mouth again and downed another long draught. It was good. Nothing was as satisfying to a real thirst as plain water.

"I guess we'd better get us something to eat now," he said. Neither of them had been able to eat while they thirsted so strongly, so they had had nothing since their morning meal.

"You bet!" Jon agreed fervently, and he began dragging foodstuffs from the grocery bag. They spread their provisions near the door for what little light was left and once more made a simple meal. Then they began to think about leaving.

"What would you think about putting all the groceries onto the plastic sheet and tying them into a bundle?" Jon asked. "I think they'd be easier to carry that way than in the sack like we had them yesterday."

"Sounds like a good idea," Benjamin agreed, and they began rearranging their belongings into two piles, one on the plastic sheet, the other on the blanket as before, then drawing up the corners and tying them into neat bundles.

"Now if we just had some good, stout sticks we could carry them over our shoulders hobo fashion," Benjamin said with a chuckle as he eyed the results of their packing.

"Hobo fashion? How's that?"

"Well, you just hook the bundle on the one end of a stick," Benjamin explained, demonstrating with his cane, "and hold it over your shoulder like this." He marched around a few steps to show how the burden was borne.

"Hey, that looks like a pretty good idea. Maybe we'll find some sticks along the way."

"Well, we might."

"Do you think it's time to go now?"

"I don't know. Let's watch for cars a little while first."

They moved to the doorway and waited. A car did come by after a few minutes, and a quarter of an hour later there came another. But then there was nothing. Minute followed minute until a half hour had gone by with nothing to be seen upon the road but one lone stray cat that wandered across from the opposite ditch. They couldn't be sure there wouldn't yet be a late traveler passing by, but they were tired of waiting and ready to take their chances. The two picked up their bundles and stumbled across the weed-cluttered barn lot to the driveway, then followed that to the edge of the road. They paused there, straining their sight as far as possible into the dark of the night. Nothing appeared, so they stepped out onto the graveled way and set their feet once more upon the pathway home.

Chapter 7

Benjamin was glad to have left the Hanson farm behind. It was a sad place, for there were enough scraps and remnants left of its former habitation to serve as constant reminders of things that had been but would be no more. At least his home was not one of the emptied, dying ones. Again he felt a great eagerness to get there.

They made good time the first hour they were out, but then their steps began to lag. At least Benjamin's did, and Jon set his pace to match the old man's. Somehow Benjamin was not so strong tonight; he tired quickly. So they began to break their march into short hitches, stopping often to rest.

Yet though his body weakened, his spirit did not. For they soon came to a grove of tall pines that crowded close to the road, and his heart swelled with the sound of their sighing music. There had been talk over the last few years of widening and paving this road, but it hadn't gotten done yet, and he was glad. He'd always enjoyed driving this portion that dipped down into the pines, and it was even more pleasureable now to walk through. He knew that there was a steep hill to climb just beyond the grove, though, and he hated to think about climbing it.

Soon they were ascending, the old man puffing as he lifted one foot after the other in short, leaden steps. They climbed in bits and dabs, working upward a little way, then stopping for Benjamin to lean on his cane and draw in some deep breaths, then trudging on again. After a while Jon silently took Benjamin's burden from his hand, and Benjamin released it without protest. On they climbed, Benjamin holding a yearning eye on the crest of the hill while Jon wished he could somehow give his old friend a boost.

At last, when it seemed to Benjamin he could go no further, the graveled roadway leveled. They had reached the top of the hill. They stopped and rested in their tracks, turning to look back over the way they had come. Now they could look down upon the tops of the pines they had passed through, could even sense that the shadowy treetops were swaying gently with the breeze, but they could no longer hear their sighs and whisperings. Beyond the treetops lay moon-blanched fields pocked here and there with a dot of light from some window. Further on lay the city and the sky above it glowed from the thousand electric fires burning below.

The city looked so far away now. Yet they were still a long way from their destination. As he thought about these distances, Benjamin felt his good spirits being swept away and replaced by a strange terror, a fear that they were caught in limbo, hopelessly remote from where they had come and equally far from where they were going.

"God, help us! Help us!" he cried inwardly in his fright. But no help seemed to come.

He stood there a while letting his weariness release great despondency until he felt he must find somewhere to sit and weep. Then he felt the boy stirring at his side.

"It's downhill for a ways now," the lad said.

"What?" Benjamin asked, not even comprehending the simple words.

"I said, it's downhill for a ways."

"Oh. Yes. Well, then—I guess we'd better go on."

He stumbled into a walk again, just putting one foot down in front of the other, and as he moved slowly down the gentle slope some of the fear drained out of him.

Eons of time seemed to pass as they descended the hill. It was not so steep on this side as it had been coming up, so walking was easier and required little effort. That was a good thing, for he had little energy left. He began to think ahead, to turn his mind to the problem of their immediate destination. Where would they spend the next daylight hours? Even though it was a good while yet until morning, he knew he must stop soon.

He tried to retrieve a picture from his memory of just where they were and what lay ahead. It was a long way down this hill; he remembered that. At the bottom were two farmhouses, one on each side of the road. A bit farther on, a quarter of a mile maybe, a small bridge came into his mind's eye. There was a creek there, a tiny stream that bisected a corn field, then ducked under the road and was swallowed up in a thicket of trees. That thicket would be a good place to spend the day. It would be cool and secluded there, with plenty of water to drink. They'd be better off than yesterday.

He set the sylvan scene as a goal, and they inched toward it, walking and resting, walking and resting. And all the while the boy moved quietly at his side, still carrying both bundles. Yet for all that load he moved more vigorously than the old man and could have gone twice as fast had he been alone. Still, he held himself back, and their snail's pace did take them forward, bit by bit, until at last they reached the bottom of the hill and passed between the two farmhouses that stood like sentinel boxes, one on each side of the road. Benjamin turned his gaze curiously to first one and then the other. He knew the Blakeleys who lived over there on the right, but the other house had new folks in it. He didn't know them. Anyway, both places were silent and dark.

All unnoticed, they left the farmhouses behind and strained onward upon the last lap of their night's journey. Finally, shining white in the moonlight, there began to show the form of the small concrete bridge up ahead. They aimed for it and kept plodding, plodding along.

Suddenly, they were there. Benjamin reached out both hands to the first concrete post he came to and leaned against it, bracing himself with the feel of its cool, sturdy form. Then, with Jon leading the way, they sat and slid down the bank that shouldered the road, stopping with a gentle bump at the bottom. They gathered themselves up and crept to the edge of the stream where, as they had hoped, a deer trail led back into the close-huddled woods. It was dark and gloomy beneath the trees, for the boughs overhead shut out all the moonlight, and they had to feel their way along, shuffling cautiously down the narrow path. They only had to go a short way to find a portion of the bank that was open enough to stretch out on, and here they lay themselves and their burdens down and rested.

They hadn't made much progress this second night, Benjamin told himself. But it couldn't be helped. He hadn't felt too pert to start with, and that big hill had done him in. Maybe tomorrow he'd do better. Anyhow, right now he wouldn't worry about it. As soon as he had had a long, cool drink of water that Jon dipped for him, he dropped off into a deep, sound slumber.

The next day was well along when he awoke. It was going to be another hot one, he could tell, so he conserved his energy, resting, snacking, dozing off into little naps, and chatting now and then with Jon. He resisted the temptation to follow the boy up and down the creek bank exploring. It was all right for him to knock about satisfying his curiosities; he could expend his energies through the heat of the day and still have plenty left for the nighttime hike. Benjamin knew he'd better stay put and save his strength. Maybe then he'd be able to cover more ground tonight.

The day in the shade of the trees rested Benjamin much better than the spell of thirst and suffocating heat in the old barn. Maybe he was getting in better shape for walking too. Anyway, the third night he held up well, and they covered almost four miles before stopping, this time to shelter in a clump of willows that bordered a big pond. He remembered when that pond had been built by damming a great gully. He'd been dubious at the time about the spring that fed it, thinking it wasn't strong enough to keep the pond filled during the summer time. It had turned out all right after all. The glistening waters that leveled the gully into a great, shining oval still lapped far up onto the bank even this late in the season. It was sure a pretty spot now. The years had lined the bank with trees and shrubbery and it seemed a perfect place to spend a warm summer day.

When the moon rose, bright and almost full, Benjamin decided they'd take a cross-country short cut. There was light enough to see by, and he knew this country well. He'd helped cut hay off these fields years ago, and he'd hunted on them several times too. He couldn't possibly lose his way, and they would save nearly two miles.

They spread apart the wires of a drooping fence and climbed through, then headed across a rolling pasture. It was a beautiful night, soft and gleaming, with an other-worldly aura shimmering over the moon-drenched fields. There was no color in this light, not a hint of the day's sun-painted golds and greens and tans, only glistening silver falling from the skies. It made for a wondrous scene, and they trod softly as they stepped across these fields of light. Once they climbed a knoll and sat down for a while just to look around.

"It's awfully pretty out tonight, isn't it?" Jon whispered after a time.

"Yes. Sure is." But discussion seemed out of place somehow, and they spoke no more until by some silent, mutual agreement they arose and went upon their way.

Benjamin was glad for the boy. It didn't matter so much about himself. He was old; he'd seen many a mystical night, moved through many a glorious day. But Jon had never known anything but city sights and sounds, and it was time he saw something of this other world. He was taking it in too, soaking up every minute. Benjamin wondered, trying to remember back to his own beginnings, what it was like to turn and see for the first time a whole circle of earth around, its form draped and shaped by all manner of growing things, and overhead the sky stretched high and wide from rim to rim. A wondrous place, this old world. It did even an old man good to get out and see something of it again, to renew his vision and freshen his joy in the grace of this bit of creation.

They clambered over and through a couple more fences, and then after a hike across another wide pasture they came to a corn field and turned aside to skirt its massive breadth. It would be too much trouble to try to wade through it; better to go around. So they walked a great angle beside the field, accompanied all the way by conversational rustlings that could be heard each time a breeze swept the rattling blades. Then the corn marched up to a fence and stopped, and they found that their shortcut had brought them back to the road again.

"Good," Benjamin said, "we came out just where I thought we would. Didn't used to be a corn field here though."

They crawled through the fence, scooted down a little bank, and found themselves at the roadside once more.

They moved on down the road and soon began descending a gentle hill that dropped into a little valley. The road continued on across the valley before turning south again, but he didn't think they would follow it all that way. They'd head off cross country again on another shortcut. He knew a good way to go, a route that skirted the edge of some wooded hills on this side of the valley and would bring them out upon the road again at a point where the valley pinched together into a draw. There would be no water accessible to them until they came to that draw, for the only stream nearby clung to the opposite side of the valley. It couldn't be more than a mile through the woods to that spot, though, and they could surely manage that.

Yet when they left the road and stepped into the first patch of woods they found the moon had withdrawn behind a cloud and left them not enough light to see by. He knew they could get through. He'd been squirrel hunting in these woods several times, and he knew they were open enough for walking. Right now it was just too dark, though, so perhaps they should settle down and wait for better light.

They felt their way along to a bit of open space that encircled the base of a giant pine and stopped there to wait. They propped their burdens against the massive trunk, then eased themselves down onto the pine-needle cushion below and sat quietly, catching their breath.

"Want a candy bar?" Jon asked after a bit, rummaging into the food parcel for the sweets.

"Yes, I guess so. Well, no, maybe not. It'll just make me thirsty."

Jon hesitated with the candy in his hand. "Maybe it'll make me thirsty too," he said, wondering, but he went ahead and unwrapped one end of it, and then he could not help but eat it. He sat silent for a few minutes afterward, and then he said in a small voice, "It did make me thirsty. How much farther is it until we come to some water?"

Benjamin smiled, for the darkness hid his amusement from the boy, and replied, "It's not so very far, but we can't get there until we get enough light to find our way through these woods."

"Yes. Well, I'll just have to wait I guess." The boy sighed his resignation and stretched out on his back, peering up into the filigree of boughs and needles that here and there allowed a star-beam to slip through. It was now very quiet in the woods, for the breeze had disappeared, and all the trees stood still as statues. Even the usual stirrings of the nocturnal creatures seemed to have subsided, and a thick silence lay over the land. The old man and the boy yielded to the mood and turned silent and still themselves until they drifted almost into sleep. Yet Benjamin, half-dozing though he was, kept his ears open, and now and then he lifted an eyelid to check for hints of morning.

Just as he began to notice the first lifting of the dark he also heard a foreign sound, a twig snapping somewhere as from the pressure of a foot. Then there came the faint crunching of dry leaves followed by the rustling of a body moving through brush. Somebody was coming!

He moved over to touch Jon's shoulder and whisper in his ear.

"Jon—be still, don't make any sound, but get back out of sight quick. Somebody's coming."

With all the stealth they could manage in their haste, they crept back into a clump of tall grass and shrubs, drawing their belongings in after them, and there they waited, almost holding their breath to be quiet. The footsteps drew nearer, paused a few moments, then came on again. Suddenly there strode into view the figure of a man, so close they could not help seeing him, and when he stopped his profile showed so plainly against the graying sky that Benjamin recognized him. There was no mistaking that long nose and jutting chin. It was Andrew Tanner, an old friend, and there was no doubt that Tanner would recognize him if he saw him. Benjamin tightened all his muscles to hold himself perfectly still for the few seconds Tanner stood in their view, and then, to his relief, the man walked on.

"I know that man," Benjamin whispered as the footsteps moved farther away.

"You do?"

"Yes. He's an old friend of mine. Has a dairy farm down there in the valley. I wonder what he's doing up here in the woods this early in the morning."

"Yeah."

For a couple of minutes longer they stayed huddled down in their hiding place. Then they began to breathe more easily.

"I don't hear him any more," Jon said. "I guess he's gone."

"Yes."

Jon raised up and stepped out into the open, moving quietly over to the great pine tree to prop one hand against it as he still listened.

Suddenly the footsteps clattered into hearing again, right close by. The man had not left the area at all; he had merely walked a little way past them, stopped to peer about and listen, then turned back. Benjamin flattened himself in the grass, but it was too late for Jon to hide again. The boy half turned as if to run, but the man was already upon him.

"Hullo!" the man grunted with surprise as he saw the boy's shape materialize in the early morning light.

"Hi," Jon managed to respond.

"You're sure out bright and early!" the man exclaimed, half questioning. Then he paused to consider a moment. "You live around here somewhere?"

"No, not very close. I'm just—hiking through the woods."

"Oh—well, it is nice to get out early like this sometimes." He paused and seemed to listen again, poised as if waiting for some clue of sound to tell him which way to go. "Say, you haven't seen a cow around here, have you?"

"No, I haven't."

"Well, I guess she didn't come this way. One of the Bartel boys was helping me around the place last evening, and he forgot and left a gate open. Might have known something like that would happen if I didn't follow around after him to see that he did things right. Anyhow, the cow got out, but I didn't notice it until it was so late I decided to let her go until morning. Now I suppose I'll have to climb on up the hill after her. She's probably gone clear to the top by now." With an air of resignation he started to walk on, angling his path toward higher ground. Then he hesitated and turned back to the boy. "Maybe you'd better be heading for home if your mother is expecting you for breakfast."

Jon didn't say anything, but he turned as if to leave.

"Well, so long," the man called after him.

"Bye." But Jon didn't go far. He walked just a little way, then stopped and waited. A long, long wait this time. Finally, he slipped back to his friend's hiding place.

"I think he really is gone this time," he whispered.

The shrubbery jerked wildly about as Benjamin grabbed hold of a limb and pulled himself up out of the cover.

"That was a close call," he said, shivering a little with fright and the cool morning air. "Too close for comfort!"

"Yeah. You said you knew him—who is that man?"

"Name's Tanner. Andrew Tanner. His farm is down at the foot of this hill. In fact, these woods are part of his place too. I've known him for a long time."

"Do you think he would have recognized you?"

"Oh, yes." Benjamin rubbed his hand over his scraggly chin and glanced with a smile down at his soiled, rumpled clothing. "Yes, he'd have sure known me, even the way I look now."

"Well then, it was a good thing it was me he ran into instead of you." Jon turned a wary glance toward Benjamin, then looked quickly away. "I didn't tell him any lies though," he said, and his voice bore a hint of question.

"No. No, you sure didn't!" Benjamin put all the approval he could muster into his tone and was gratified to see the boy visibly relax and straighten his back into an attitude of assurance.

"Do you think we ought to go now?" Jon asked after a moment.

"Yes, let's get on out of here before Tanner comes back down the hill. We'd better hustle too. He's liable to be roaming all over the place until he finds that cow," Benjamin chuckled. "He always did have a lot of trouble keeping his stock in. It's a wonder he didn't try to recruit you to help him look for her."

"Well, he seemed to think I ought to be heading for home instead."

"Yes, I heard. He probably thought it was a little strange to find somebody out here this time of day." Benjamin picked up his bundle and started threading his way through the trees. "Let's get off of his place. I think I know where we can spend the day."

They hurried along then, anxious to reach their destination, and they did make good time, for the hill soon began to slope gently down to the draw, and walking here was easy. Soon they were able to lay their burdens down once more beside a tiny stream, drink their fill, and stretch out upon a shaded bank to rest. They'd done well this night, Benjamin told himself, had covered a lot of ground. If their luck held a couple of days longer they'd make it home all right. Yes, he began to feel sure they were going to make it.

Benjamin's sense of satisfaction held as they waited out the daytime hours, eating when they were hungry, sleeping when they felt like it, exploring a little way up and down the creek. And when nightfall came they were ready to go again.

They took up their bundles and maneuvered their way along the stream until they reached the roadside, then scrambled up the graveled shoulder to put their feet upon the winding roadway once more.

All went well again this night. They held to the road the entire time, for there were no shortcuts here that would help them. They walked and rested, walked and rested. A car did slip up behind them once when there was no place to seek cover, but they kept walking in as relaxed a manner as they could, and the car flew on past without pause.

By the time they climbed to the top of the last little hill that Benjamin felt he could manage, he was well satisfied with their progress. They were drawing close to their goal. From this hilltop it was only about four more miles, one night's walk. Just think—by this time tomorrow he might be stepping onto his own sod!

Right now he needed to find a place for them to spend the day, and he thought he knew just the place.

"See that?" he said to Jon as off to the right side of the road they approached a tall structure gleaming softly white in the moonlight.

"What is this place?" Jon whispered as their feet crunched up the graveled drive. "Does somebody live here?"

"No. It's a church. There won't be anybody around this time of the week though, so I thought it would be a good place for us to stay."

Benjamin climbed the steps and tried the front door, but it was locked. He turned and reached up on a ledge at the left side of the porch, and smiled as his fingers touched a key.

"Not very burglar-proof," he said. "Used to be it was never locked at all."

Benjamin inserted the key in the door and it easily opened. The pair stepped inside and pushed the door gently shut behind them.

It was the same as always. He could not see much yet, but the old familiar smells struck him full in the face. They were good odors, fragrances of old wood and varnish, of hidden dust lying long undisturbed, of the faint lingerings of soaps and perfumes used by a long succession of worshippers. All added up to a wholesome churchly aroma, an incense of the piety of innumerable Sunday services, and when he drew in a full breath it brought him a pang of nostalgia so sharp that it hurt.

He turned his attention away and moved toward a tiny kitchen that he knew was tucked away in a corner.

"Should be a sink right over here," he murmured as he pushed open the door. Yes, there it was, the white of the porcelain shining in the middle of the counter top. He felt around for the faucet, took a paper cup from the nearby dispenser, filled it, and handed it to Jon to drink. Then it was his turn, and then Jon's again, until their thirst was quenched.

"You went to church here, did you?" Jon asked, as they moved back into the sanctuary.

"Yes, this was my church. Still is for that matter, but of course I haven't had a chance to attend services here for a long time. Used to come every Sunday though, and all my family too. We usually sat right there about three rows back, and when all the kids were home we pretty near filled up a whole pew." He smiled, picturing in his mind how they must have looked.

"Is it all right for us to be here?" Jon said. "I mean—would anybody mind?"

"Why, no—don't think so. This is my church. I even helped build it about—oh, close to forty years ago I guess it was. I know all the members, and they all know me. They sure wouldn't mind if I came in to get a drink and rest awhile. I'm practically a fixture around here, kind of a pillar of the church, you might say!"

They sat silent then for a little while, watching the plain glass windows brighten as faint hints of daylight began to show through. Then Benjamin turned again to the boy.

"Do you ever go to church, Jon?"

"Naw. Well, I did go to Sunday School for a while when I was little. But I decided I didn't like it and quit." The boy held his next words back for a moment, but then he went ahead and blurted them out. "You see, I don't believe much in God!"

"You don't? Why not, Jon?"

The boy shifted about in the pew, perhaps uneasy about making a statement of unbelief right in a church building. But he would say what he thought, and when he spoke it came out honestly.

"Well—if there was a God, and if He was all-powerful like they say He is—well, He just wouldn't let bad things happen, would He?" The childish treble dropped to a troubled whisper then. "He wouldn't have—let those bad things happen to me— like He did."

So. It was the age-old problem, the question that had troubled men from the times of the ancients until today.

"Well, but, Jon—it wasn't God that hurt you, you know. It was your mother."

"Yes, but He let her, didn't He? And if He is so powerful and can do anything, why did He let her?"

"Because He limits His power when it comes to us human beings. He doesn't make us do things His way all the time. He lets us choose."

"You mean choose between right and wrong?"

"Yes. God gave man a free will so he could decide things for himself. Of course God wants us to choose to do His will—to do good—but He doesn't force us to."

"So you don't think God can keep somebody from doing bad things if they want to?"

"Well, He might take away the opportunity for doing something bad. But, no, He won't force us to do only good things. We can always choose to do bad."

"Hmm." Jon thought for a few moments and then spoke again. "Well, it looks to me like God could have made things better than that. Looks to me like He should have made people so they wouldn't do wrong."

"But then they wouldn't have any choice. They would have no will of their own."

"Well, if they only did good, wouldn't that be better?"

"Would it be better to be just a puppet? With no will of your own?"

Jon sat silent and wrestled with this one for a bit. "Well, maybe not. I don't know."

Benjamin smiled and placed his hand on the boy's shoulder with a gentle squeeze.

"Well, I don't know all there is to know about it either, Jon. Nobody does. But I believe that God is good, and so He must have had a good reason for making us free to decide things for ourselves."

They turned silent for a while then, each busy with his own thoughts. They watched as more and more light seeped through the windows to illumine the shapes and outlines of the small church sanctuary and its furnishings. Lined up properly were ten pews on each side with an aisle down the middle. At the end of the aisle stood a big box of a pulpit and behind it were three pews nestled into a tiny choir loft. His daughter, Mary, had begun singing in the choir as soon as she was old enough, and he could picture her there now, standing amid the sopranos letting her sweet, clear voice ring out on the hymns. She'd loved to sing and had turned out to be the only one in his family with a really good voice.

He turned his attention back to the pew on which he was sitting. Yes, it was the same old one. All these pews had been bought slightly used when the building was first put up, and they'd been in pretty fair shape then. But they were beginning to look battered and worn now. A lot of years of scrapes and scratches and even a few carved initials had taken their toll.

He remembered one set of initials, a "T" and a "W," with a

twinge of pain. They'd been scratched on the farthest back pew on this side, and it was his own son who had put them there. He'd figured out when he first noticed the freshly carved letters that there weren't any other boys in Sunday School at the time with those initials, so he'd been pretty sure who the culprit was.

And Timothy had owned up to it when accosted with the evidence. You had to give the boy credit for that. Most of the time he'd been a good boy, really. Benjamin couldn't imagine what had gotten into him that he'd pulled a stunt like that. He'd taken his punishment well though, and Benjamin had dealt out a hard licking too, one of the few times he'd resorted to that. Then he'd made arrangements for Tim to do the yard work around the church all one summer to pay for the damage he'd done. And it had seemed to have a good effect on him, for he'd never indulged in anything bordering on vandalism again.

Yes, he had been a good kid, a bit mischievous maybe, but good. As good a son as a father could ask for. Now it hurt Benjamin all over again to think about the punishment he'd inflicted. He wondered if he'd have had the courage to do it if he'd known Timothy was going to be killed in that car accident just a few years later. Maybe not. Still, the boy had had it coming, and you had to do what seemed right at the time.

He sighed and wrenched his thoughts away from the pain of remembering about Timothy. It was good to think of this son sometimes, to keep him in his place in the memories of good family times, but it did not do to dwell on the remembrance of losing him.

It was the same way with Kate. He liked to remember her— she was never far out of his thoughts really—but he placed her always back in the good times, never, if he could help it, in the period of her illness and death. A man could only stand so much. So when he drew her image forth from his store of recollections it was nearly always a young, happy one. Her face, tanned and freckled and framed in crisp, brown hair, would come to him with a quick, wide smile, and it comforted him to see her thus.

She had always complained that her mouth was too big, but he'd never thought it so. He'd relished the sight of her with her mouth thrown wide in free, joyous laughter, for she'd been a vigorous, happy woman and had made things lively for them all. He wondered if Steven and Janet and Mary remembered those good times too. He supposed they did now and then, but of course they were busy and had their own affairs to think about now, and they probably didn't spend so much time reminiscing about the old days as he did.

Yet now he grew weary, even of his memories. He was tired not only from the long walk but also from the strain of all the remembering this old church house had brought him. Best put such things out of his mind and get some sleep. He glanced down at Jon and saw that his eyes were getting heavy too, so he got up and moved to the pew behind to give the boy more room to stretch out.

"Are you hungry?" Jon's voice piped to him after he had laid himself down.

"No. No, I just want to rest right now. Get yourself something if you want to though."

He closed his eyes and listened as the boy rattled around in a grocery bag. Then he heard the faint grinding of a can opener working around the rim of a can. He smelled something fishy, tuna probably or salmon. Funny that the smell of food didn't spur his appetite. Maybe he was too tired. He'd eat later. He turned to fit his back into the curve of the wooden bench, and then, cradled in the hard comfort of the old church pew, he fell asleep.

Chapter 8

It was with a bit of sadness that Benjamin pushed the door shut and locked it behind him as they left the church that evening. Who could tell; he might never see the place again.

He pushed these feelings away and turned his thoughts to the night's journey ahead. Eagerness seized him and hurried his steps as they crunched down the gravel driveway to the road. They were approaching home territory now, and if all went well they might make it to his farm by the very next morning!

They marched steadily down the road, and his heart lifted with the passing of each familiar milestone. First there was the Cantrell place, then the Turners' and the Hammonds'. Then they came to the little bridge over Horse Creek. Benjamin leaned against the railing of the bridge to catch his breath a moment and turned to peer down into the stream. Best he could tell, there was an unusually large amount of water in it for this late in the season. That meant that the creek on his property should also have plenty of water, and fishing should be good. He could hardly wait to drop a line into one of his old fishing holes, and with that anticipation there came an urgency that pushed him off the railing and back onto the road again.

But somehow, eager as he was to get home, he just didn't have any endurance tonight. Perhaps everything was catching up with him. Perhaps he had used up the little strength left in his old body. He tried to reject the thought and pressed on doggedly, but found himself stopping more and more often for rest. After a while it seemed they were resting as much as they were walking. Yet after each stop he forced himself to lift up his burdens again and press on, until after what must have been his tenth or fifteenth or twentieth stop, Jon took the old man's burden as well as his own.

Gradually the terrain fell behind them as they worked themselves farther on and higher up. Though it made for hard going, this stretch of rough country was a stimulant to Benjamin's spirit, for he had a great affection for this land, stressed and riven as it was. It was only the more beautiful to him for that, and it was near his place. They would climb and climb until they came out onto the great broad hilltop that bore the Erickson pasture right up to his own boundary line. And then they would be home.

Benjamin pushed and pushed himself until they stood at last at the bottom of that final hill. Day had come. It had been slipping up on them for the last hour, gradually lighting the road before them to ease their way. Yet it was also exposing them to plain view. Benjamin didn't know whether to go on or not.

"We could hide out in those trees over there," Jon volunteered, and he pointed out a clump of oaks that straddled a rock-filled gully nearby. "We could wait there until night comes again."

"Yes, I suppose we could," Benjamin replied. But he hated the thought of settling down to wait out the tedious hours of another long day. Not when they were this close to home. No, he just couldn't do it. He had to go on.

"I think we'll try to make it on up the hill," he said, making his decision, "but not by the road. We'll cut across houses on that side, and unless somebody is hiking around, we're not likely to be seen. I think we'll chance it anyhow."

"Good!" Jon grinned his anticipation. "We're almost to your farm now, aren't we?"

"Yes. Yes, we're almost there." And with the encouragement of his own words, Benjamin grasped his cane firmly and shoved himself forward again.

Slowly they forced their way up the vast slope, lifting themselves a step at a time and sometimes only an inch or two at a step. For the hill extruded rocks and stumps and bushes to block their way, and they had to bend their path often to go around these obstacles. Their efforts seemed minute, like the wrigglings of two ants upon a mountainside, and yet they kept moving, first this way and then that, and always upward when they could. Finally they found they had wormed their way to what from below had appeared to be about the halfway mark, a giant pine that propped up a needle-strewn ledge against the hillside, and here they flung themselves down for a rest.

"Can we make it—the rest of the way—do you think?" Jon panted after a bit.

"I don't know," Benjamin admitted after a long silence of hard breathing. "I know you could. I'm not so sure about me."

"Maybe I could help you somehow," Jon ventured after a few moments of consideration.

"I don't know—how you could help me—any more than you are already," Benjamin said, and it was true. Jon was helping him a great deal. Not only had he been carrying both bundles, but whenever they came to a particularly difficult spot he had carried them on ahead, then returned to lend Benjamin a steadying hand.

"Well," Jon began again after a few more minutes' thought, "how would it be if I took all our stuff on up to the top and left it there and then came back to help you?"

"Jon, you'd have to climb the hill twice that way."

"Yes, but I don't mind. I'm really almost doing that anyway. I think it would be easier to take everything on up than to be having to pick things up and set them down all the time."

Benjamin was ashamed to realize that this was true. He was being an awful lot of trouble to the boy. It angered him so to know this that in his weariness he almost wept.

"I hate being such a burden to you!" he suddenly cried out. "I don't know why I have to be so old and weak and clumsy!"

Jon was startled at this outburst and turned wide and pained eyes upon his friend.

"Why, I didn't mean—you're not a burden to me!" he protested.

"Yes, I am! Don't try to say otherwise, I know that I am!" Benjamin turned and lay face down, pressing his forehead against his arm to hide the sight of his agony from the boy. He knew he was breaking down, and he hated doing it, but he couldn't seem to stop.

"Well, so what!" Jon cried out, and now he was upset too. "So what if I have to help you a little! You've helped me, haven't you? You've helped me do lots of things. Why can't I help you a little?"

Benjamin held himself quiet for a long moment as the boy's words sank in. He knew Jon was right. There was no reason for him to throw a fit because of infirmities he couldn't help. A man ought to be able to accept a little help when it was needed without getting his back up about it. It was just his foolish pride getting him all worked up, and he'd better take himself in hand and quit behaving so childishly. He stirred and made himself sit up, but he couldn't face Jon, not yet.

"I'm sorry," he mumbled with eyes averted to one side. "I didn't mean to go to pieces like that. You're right, there's nothing the matter with your helping me. I appreciate it—I really do."

"Well—I appreciate things you've done for me too. If it wasn't for you . . . " Jon's words trailed off, and they both sat in silence for a long while. Then Benjamin turned and faced the boy again with a calm countenance.

"I think your idea—about taking our stuff on up to the top of the hill—was a good one," he said. "Why don't you go ahead and do that whenever you feel rested enough."

"Well—if you want me to. Are you—going to stay here?"

"Yes, I'll wait right here until you get back."

"Okay."

Jon crept back and forth on his knees gathering up things, and then he got to his feet, ready to leave. Yet he turned one more troubled glance to his friend before starting.

"I'm all ready, I guess," he said, hesitating.

"All right. You might try to find some kind of hiding place for those things when you get up there," Benjamin said, "a clump of bushes or something." He was making normal conversation now and trying to put some cheer into his voice. He could tell he needed to reassure the boy a little.

"Okay, I will." Jon hitched one bundle more firmly up into his grasp, then turned to go. "Well—I'll see you."

For a moment there could be heard the scufflings of Jon's

feet as he scrambled over a rocky stretch to begin his climb. But soon he was out of hearing, and all was quiet. Very quiet. Benjamin was glad. He needed a spell of aloneness right now, a chance to gather himself together and get a better grip on things. He didn't know why he'd begun to come apart at the seams like that. Funny, for he'd never been an emotional type, not one to get upset over little things. No doubt it was the strain of this long journey. It had been harder on him than he'd realized. He was awfully tired, he knew that, and hungry and thirsty. This big hill was enough to discourage anybody. Perhaps they should have stopped and waited out the day down there in the gully after all. But he'd wanted so desperately to set his feet on his own sod this very day. Maybe he'd do it yet! He was halfway up this hill now, and he just might make it the rest of the way. He'd certainly try, no matter how long it took! But those kinds of thoughts stirred his anger at his weakness again, and he began to tremble inwardly with the fervor of his emotion.

"No," he muttered, gritting his teeth, "I mustn't let myself get worked up again. I won't! What in the world is the matter with me anyway?"

He drew his knees up and clasped his arms around them to get the feel of holding on to himself. Then he dropped his head to his knees and waited for the calmness to begin. He prayed, mostly just thinking about God and asking for help to conduct himself like he should, and for strength to climb the hill. That was all he could think of. Seemed it was hard for him to collect his thoughts for serious praying or thinking sometimes. Even so, an ease gradually flowed into him that undid the kinks and settled the shakiness inside. He had to quit railing against the way things were, Benjamin told himself. He was old. There was no changing that. He wasn't going to be able to do the things a young man could do, or even what this child could do. He mustn't blame himself for his weakness. Certainly his age and the illness he'd suffered were in no way his fault. There was nothing for him to feel guilty about. These things just happened to people. Why shouldn't they happen to him? He was no different from anybody else. There was no reason for him to be spared all troubles and difficulties while others suffered. Nobody had been promised immunity like that. A man had to live with what came, and not throw childish fits whenever things didn't go his way. Maybe he should think, too, a little more about the good things that had come his way lately. Like getting out of the Home, now that had been good. Finding Jon—that had been about the best thing that had happened to him in a long while. Their days together at the park had been full of good times. Even this long journey, tedious and filled with struggle as it had been, had offered times of beauty and joy, and constant good companionship. There would be more good things to come, he knew, if he could just get up this hill and make it on home.

He sighed and turned his eyes again upon the forbidding slope. He hadn't remembered it was so steep on this side. Perhaps after all they would have done better to have stayed with the road and taken their chances on being seen and recognized. It wasn't nearly as hard a climb from the road to the top of the hill as it had turned out to be over here. Well, no use thinking about that now. They were here, and he had to get up this side of the hill or face an awfully long detour around.

As he swept his eyes across the slope, searching for what might be the easiest way up, he saw a figure come flying over the crest of the hill and start half-running, half-sliding toward him. He was startled for a moment, but it was only Jon. The boy slowed his pace some as he continued his maneuvers down the hillside, but it was only a couple of minutes until he had pulled to a halt at Benjamin's side.

"Well—I made it!" he announced happily. "All the way—to the top!"

"Did you find a place to stash our belongings?"

"Yes. There's a great big pile of old limbs and stuff right near where I came out on top, and I hid our things under that. Nobody would ever see them unless they practically walked into the brush pile."

"Sounds like a good place." Benjamin stopped and tugged at his memory a minute. Seemed he remembered a brush pile. He recollected the Ericksons clearing some land for pasture a few years back. They'd left behind a pile of debris that they'd never gotten around to burning. Yes, that was it, and it should make a good hiding place for their things until Jon could get him the rest of the way up the hill.

"Well, if you're rested enough I'd better stir these old legs so we can get at it again," he said, bracing himself against the tree trunk with his hand as he forced himself back up to his feet and turned toward the steep incline before him. Then, as he looked up, he almost couldn't face it. It was too much. He had spent himself. There was nothing left in him for this last climb. As he stood there hesitating, his mind replayed their past strivings. He saw again the endless strips of road that had stretched before them. He felt the jolt of the rocks and ruts he had stumbled over and the pricks of barbed wires and brambles. He suffered the heat of the day and the chill of the night. He felt a deep weariness from all the moods that had swept him, both the exhilaration of his revelings in the vast, free countryside and the depression of the discouragements and fears that had taken hold of him and shaken him so hard at times. Now he just needed peace and rest and an end to all contending against both the world about and his own humors. He needed a time of ease. He did not need another difficult, strenuous climb. Yet there stood the hill still before him.

"Is it a long way to the top?" he asked wistfully, hoping that Jon would reassure him that it wasn't far. But his hope was in vain.

"Yes, it's pretty far," the boy replied. "And it gets steep in places too."

Benjamin gazed up at the slope again, and he felt a weakness start at the soles of his feet and rise up like sap through him until the remnants of his strength were watered down even more.

"I don't think I can do it," he murmured at last.

"But—we've got to get up there. Haven't we?" A note of fear came into Jon's voice. If Benjamin failed him all would be lost.

"Yes—but right now I just don't think I can. . . . "

"Well, maybe if we just went a little way and then rested some more. See that big, white rock over there? Do you think you could make it that far?"

"Well—maybe."

"Okay. Let's try it." Jon stepped beside his friend and put an arm across his back, while Benjamin's hand dropped down to the boy's shoulder, and together they moved off, shuffling slowly and haltingly the first few steps. Once Benjamin got going again he seemed to strengthen a bit. Yet he was more than ready to sit down on the rock by the time they reached it, and as he rested he wiped the perspiration from his brow with a shaking hand.

"It's getting hot already," he murmured, glancing with resentment at the sky.

"Yes. Wish we had some shade."

They waited five minutes, then ten. Finally John stirred uneasily and touched his hand to Benjamin's arm.

"Do you think you can go on now?" he asked.

"I don't know. Let me rest just a little longer."

"But it's so hot here. It might not be doing you any good to stay out here in the sun so long. Why don't we try to get on up to another tree? How about that one—right over there."

"Well—all right." Still Benjamin didn't move until Jon tugged a little at his arm. Then he struggled to his feet again and shoved off in the direction Jon pointed.

It was the same as before. At first it was hard to get himself going, but once underway he drew from somewhere a tiny spurt of energy that carried him forward a little way. They made it to the tree. But once there and settled gratefully in the shade, Benjamin decided he wasn't going to let Jon budge him for a while.

Yet Jon was not easily dissuaded.

"We can't stay here very long," he pleaded. "It's going to be real hot today, and there's no water anywhere on this hillside. At least I haven't seen any."

"No, there isn't any near here."

"Well, aren't you getting thirsty?"

"Yes, a little bit." But his weariness was greater than his thirst, and he didn't move.

"Well, then—what do you want to do?"

"Just rest for a while. I need to rest."

So Jon gave up his urgings and sat down beside Benjamin. Yet he couldn't stay settled long, for he was uneasy about their situation, and in a short time he had bounced back to his feet and was pacing restlessly, sweeping his gaze back and forth across the lands below as if searching for something. Finally he dropped back to his knees beside Benjamin, who lay half-propped up against the tree trunk.

"Do you want to stay here all day?" he asked. "Just wait here until it gets cool again in the evening?"

Benjamin tried to think. For a moment the old craving to plant his feet on his own land seized him again, and he felt he couldn't bear to waste a whole day sitting here under a tree. Then his weariness struck him down again. He couldn't climb any more of that hill. Not now. He had to have more rest first. So with an effort he lifted his head and spoke to the anxious eyes peering at him.

"I don't know, Jon," he said. "But I can't go any farther right now. I'm sorry, but I just can't."

Jon looked away for a moment into the rugged lands below. Then he turned back to question his friend.

"All right then, I guess we'd better stay here," he said. "But we need to find some water. It will be awfully hard to go all day without something to drink. Do you know if there are any streams in any of those gullies down there? Any close enough for me to get to?"

Benjamin tried to think about it, but it was hard. He knew this country well. He should know if there were a drop of water anywhere around, but he couldn't seem to concentrate. He sat up and struggled to organize his recollection of their surroundings.

First, he eyed the gully at the bottom of the hill. They had crossed over it to begin their climb, and it had been bone dry, which wasn't surprising this time of year. It usually had a little water in it through the winter and spring months, but not in the summertime. He tried to trace its course in his mind. Surely it ran into something farther down the line, perhaps a stream that might still hold water. But as far as he could picture the gully winding through the hills it held to its solitary way and joined no other. Perhaps it just flattened out at last and lost itself down in the Ericksons' lower pasture. He couldn't remember, but he was pretty sure there wasn't much hope of its producing any water.

Well then, where else might they find some? He set himself to considering each feature of the semi-circle of landscape before them. Did that little valley off to the east mark the course of a year-round stream? Did another one a bit farther on cradle a pond? Did any nearby hillside bear a spring? He couldn't remember any. Did that row of distant trees mark a creek bank? No, he was sure it was just a hedgerow. And so it went. When he had mapped everything out in his mind as clearly as he could, he found no water. He sank back discouraged.

"I can't think of a thing," he announced after a moment. "There just isn't any water down there."

"Well, what about the other side of the hill?"

"You mean this hill?"

"Yes."

"Well, sure there's a good creek down in the valley over there. Runs across my property. But it's a long way from here. Too far to go and carry water back. I'd be afraid for you to try to find it by yourself."

"I guess we're just going to have to tough it out again then, huh?" asked Jon in a small voice.

"I'm afraid so." Benjamin sighed and thought back to the day they'd spent in the barn, remembering how they'd suffered from thirst. He hated for them to have to go through another day like that. But perhaps there was no way out of it.

Then suddenly the picture of a pump flashed into his mind, an ancient pump standing beside the crumbling bricks of an old chimney. Of course! Why hadn't he thought of it sooner? On top of the ridge and west a ways was the old Kennerly place. The Kennerlys had settled there long ago and had tried to farm that end of the ridge, but they'd never had much success on the thin, rocky soil, and finally they'd given up and sold out to the Ericksons. Harlan Erickson had turned the land back into pasture and had torn down the little house for lumber to build a barn. All that was left was the old foundation, a crumbling chimney, and the well and pump. It was a good well, and he felt sure the pump was still working. Many a time he'd used it himself to get a drink whenever he happened to be over that way, and it had always yielded plenty of good water. Wasn't very far from here either. Exuberant at his recollection, he sat up and turned eagerly to Jon.

"I've got it! Go back up the hill and turn right when you get to the top. Then follow the ridge about a quarter of a mile to where it bends a little toward the south. Right there at the bend is a little grove of firs, and just the other side of those trees you'll find a foundation where there used to be a house."

"There isn't any house there now?"

"No, just a foundation and a crumbling chimney. Right there near the chimney is a well with a pump. You ought to be able to get water out of it unless somebody's taken the pump out, and I don't think they have. It's been there a long time."

"Okay. I think I can find it all right."

"You'd better stop where you left our things and get the coffee pot to take along so you'll have something to carry the water in."

"All right, I will." Jon jumped eagerly to his feet and took a few steps up the hill. But then he hesitated and turned back to his friend. "You're going to wait right here for me, aren't you?"

"Yes, I sure am," Benjamin replied with a feeble grin. "I'm too tired to go wandering around. Do you think you can find your way back to this spot okay?"

"Yes." But Jon looked across the surrounding hillside a moment and hesitated. It was a great span of countryside, and he was not familiar with it. But then he decided what to do. "I can follow the ridge back to where that brush pile is, and then I'll know that is the place to start downhill."

"Yes, that should work out all right."

"Well—see you later." Jon gave a little wave of the hand and took another tentative step up the hill.

"Okay. Hurry back," Benjamin said with an encouraging nod, and then he watched as the child climbed once more up the steep hillside, his thin legs pumping hard to lift him up and up until he grew tiny to Benjamin's view and disappeared over the crest. When he could no longer see the boy, Benjamin sighed and sank back against the tree.

As he waited, it was hard not to let his mind dwell too much on the forthcoming drink of water, for he had nothing else to do, and his thirst was becoming intense. At last he forced his thoughts to a memory of a happy time he'd had up there on the ridge years ago, when he'd brought Timothy and Steven to help him cut wood there. It was all a good memory, one so pleasant that by the time he relived it in his mind he forgot all his present discomfort and dropped off to sleep.

He dozed and dreamed for a long while with the heavy heat of the midday pressing him into a state of torpid helplessness. He lay still as one dead, yet all the while his dreaming mind wandered about among recollections of days long gone by. Thus the minutes and the hours slipped by until finally a burst of sunshine slid beneath the leaves overhead to settle squarely upon his face, burning his cheeks and blistering his eyelids. The discomfort became so great that he roused himself and with a few feeble grunts drew back from the searching rays into a still shaded spot. There he lay for a few minutes until he more thoroughly woke up, and as he did so he became intensely aware that his thirst had now grown to much less manageable proportions. In fact, it was hard to think of anything else but this one craving. He would sure be glad when Jon got back with that water.

He glanced up the hill to see if Jon had come in sight yet, but all the scene his eye could reach was empty. Seemed the boy had been gone quite awhile. Surely he would be coming soon. Suddenly it came to him that the sun had dropped so low in the sky that it must be getting very late, only an hour or a bit more until sundown. He'd slept longer than he'd realized. There was no possible reason for Jon to have taken this long to go to the well and back, even tired as the little fellow doubtless was, unless something had happened to delay him. Alarmed, Benjamin scrambled to his feet and, clutching at the tree trunk to steady himself, looked hard at each portion of the hillside, then raised his eyes to sweep the crest of the ridge as far as he could see. Nothing stirred anywhere. Something had gone wrong, no doubt about it.

He wondered what to do. Here he was, stuck on this hillside, with Jon off somewhere probably needing help and he unable to do anything about it. Yet he must! It was he who had sent the boy off alone like that. He was responsible if the boy had gotten into some kind of trouble. He wondered what could have happened. It had seemed a fairly simple thing for Jon to do, just climb the hill, then follow his directions to the pump and return. He should have been able to find his way all right. What could possibly have gone wrong? Whatever it was, he'd better try to get himself up on this hill and find out.

He pushed himself away from the tree and took a few steps to test his strength. Good, he felt better than he'd expected. The long rest had done him good. His legs held firm once more, and his steps went straight and steady. All right then, he should be up to doing some climbing again. It would be hazardous going it alone, but he'd manage. He'd be very careful.

He started off heading straight up the hill, but quickly realized it was too hard going that way. So he turned and began to work his way back and forth, reducing the climb to more gentle grades. Gradually he maneuvered his way farther and farther up. His middle felt lean with hunger and his mouth was dry with thirst, but he didn't bother about that now. He thought only about getting up the hill and finding Jon. He turned his eyes often to the ridge to see if the boy's form might appear, but it did not. He looked as frequently to the sun to see whether he would make it to the top before sundown. He hoped to. But he didn't. He was a good way short of the crest when the last tiny, red rim sank out of sight. He knew the daylight would linger, and he'd have no trouble finding his way, but he also needed time to find Jon before dark. On and on he urged himself, driven by concern for the child. When dusk at last began to settle close about him he staggered, panting and quivering, out onto level ground.

"Ah-h-h-h!" He gave a long sigh of relief when he looked about and saw where he was. He'd done it! He'd made it all the way to the top. Under his own steam too! He grabbed at a small sapling for support, and as he steadied himself he swept his gaze all along the fading western horizon and up into the darkening sky. Yes, the great hill lay all beneath his feet. His exultation was such that it might have been the top of the world on which he stood.

His eyes began to search out the land between the spot

where he stood and the stand of firs he'd given Jon for a landmark. It was getting too dark to see much. He'd have to head in that direction for a closer look.

Tentatively he released his hold on the tree, and he wobbled a bit as it sprang away from his grasp. His feet held firm beneath him, however, and as he began to step gingerly along he found the ground smooth and level, and he had no difficulty except that he was tired now. The climb had stretched his energies thin, and he would have thought he couldn't go on without resting except that his anxiety about the boy pushed him on. He pressed forward, stopping every few steps to peer about in the gathering gloom and to call the child's name.

Suddenly to his weakening call there came an answering shout. A few seconds later a weaving, bobbing figure came bounding out of the dusk toward him. It was Jon, reaching something toward him with both hands. Benjamin raised his own hands to meet the boy's, to grasp and hold in them the coffee pot half filled with water.

"I'm sorry it's not fuller, but I spilled some on the way," Jon apologized.

"Doesn't matter, it's enough," Benjamin murmured after taking several great swallows. He dropped the rim of the pot an inch or so from his lips to take a long breath and then pressed it back again and drank deeply once more. A cool, freshening feeling moved down his throat as the water sank into his parched body, and he heaved a great sigh of satisfaction.

"I'm sorry I didn't get back with the water sooner," Jon continued his worried apology. "I know you must be awful thirsty."

"It's okay. I wasn't too bad off. Not as bad as that day in the barn. But what happened to keep you so long? I was getting worried."

"Oh, it was a bunch of girls."

"Girls?"

"Yeah, a bunch of dumb girls and some woman with them. They were on a hike, I guess. Maybe they were Girl Scouts or something. Anyway, just after I found the pump and got me a drink, I heard these people talking, and it sounded like they were real close by, so I ran back to those trees and hid. In a minute I could see them coming, so I climbed up one of those trees that's real bushy. They went right to the pump and stopped there to get water, and then they sat around and had a picnic. I thought they'd never leave."

"But they're gone now?"

"Yes, they finally left when it began to get late, and then I came down from the tree and went to the pump again and got you some water. Say, how did you get up here? I thought you were going to wait for me."

"Well, I did wait a long time. Then I began to get a little worried because you were gone so long, so I decided to come on up here and see if I could find you." Benjamin hesitated a bit, then spoke again in a sheepish tone. "Besides, I'd kind of got my strength back by then. Wasn't any need to keep lying around." His weakness embarrassed him still, and the remembrance of his breakdown in composure forced his voice to a whisper. "I don't know why I fizzled out so bad on you there for a while."

"Why, you couldn't help it! You couldn't help getting tired and worn out."

"Well, maybe not. But still . . . " Benjamin's voice trailed off, away from the painful topic. Then he turned from Jon's side and moved a couple of steps in the direction where he remembered his fence line to be. But he could no longer see it. It was getting too dark. "Are we far from the fence here, Jon? Do you remember seeing it when you came this way before?"

"Yes, it's right over there a little way, just the other side of that big rock."

"Well, I was wondering—I don't want to go much farther, but maybe we could get on over to my side of the fence before we stop for the night. It'd be kind of nice to spend the night on my own land—since we're this close. But we've got to retrieve our packs too."

"Sure, we can do that. Easy." Jon was to the brush pile and back in just a few minutes and led off then, Benjamin at his side, bracing himself again with one arm across the boy's shoulder. After a short walk they came up against four strands of barbed wire. Benjamin put out a hand to test the top one. It was still firm and taut. Looked like the fence was holding up well. Showed he'd done a good job of it when he put it in twelve—maybe fifteen—years ago. He gave the wire a final tug of satisfaction, then bent down to check the middle and bottom strands, wondering if they would spread enough to let him climb through. Yes, he thought so, if Jon would hold them apart. Seeing the need, Jon pressed his foot on a lower wire, then pulled up with all his might on the next above, and slowly, carefully, Benjamin worked his way between them.

Jon quickly popped through after him, and they both straightened and turned to look out across the darkening valley before them. Benjamin couldn't see much in this light. But what he could see, he knew. Every knobby hill his eyes could form in the dusk was a familiar shape. Every fir that lifted its peaked top into the evening skyline was an old friend. Off to the right there, pricking through the heavy dark laid down by the pines, was the twinkling of a light from the house. Next to it there flashed another that came and went quickly as from the opening and closing of a door. That would be the barn. Seemed the Bentons were a little late getting their evening chores done. If it had been Benjamin now, he'd have been finished and back up to the house by this time. But never mind about that. The barn was there; the house was there. And the people were there. All was as it ever had been. A great sense of relief swept through him. Everything was all right. As he stood and gazed out over his beloved land a joy swelled up so full within him that it spilled over in a few silent tears that trickled down his weathered cheeks. He had finished his course. The odyssey was done. He was home.

Chapter 9

The days that followed on Benjamin's farm were an idyl. Early the first morning Benjamin led Jon down the hill to the creek, and there they romped away the whole of the day, bathing, swimming, drinking and soaking up their fill of the good, clear water. The heat of the midday sun was no torment to them but rather a blessing, for it brought the warmth that gave comfort in splashing into the chill of the waters. Slowly they made their way downstream, exploring one pool after another and then climbing out onto the bank to dry and sun themselves.

Benjamin was a boy again. He took the same joy in the sparkling water as did Jon, except that where Jon was seeing each bend and pool and tiny rapid for the first time, Benjain was renewing old acquaintance. It was with the pleasure of a child that he pointed out to his friend the good fishing holes, the great flat rocks that forded the stream in several places, the deer trails that wound down to the water's edge, and three shallow caves that sank back into a small, overhanging bluff.

It was in one of these caves, the largest, that they decided to make their home. It was a good place, as Benjamin knew, dry and sheltered, with a handy spot for a seculded fire near the opening. There were even charred bite of wood and ashes at the crude fireplace already. Benjamin wondered who had built the last fire there, and when. His own young ones had come here often, but that had been long ago. He suspected that other neighborhood children had explored these caves periodically since, and they had probably built fires and picnicked too. He hoped no one would come around while he and Jon were here, but if someone did perhaps he could just say they were on a camping trip. That was true enough, goodness knows. He'd been on a camping trip ever since he'd left the Home. My, how long ago that seemed now. A lot had happened since then. A bit of pride swelled within him as he thought about his accomplishments. He'd gotten away from that prison and he'd stayed away. He may have had his problems, but he'd managed—with Jon's help—to get along on his own for quite a long while now. Yes, he'd done all right. He'd made himself a free man and gotten back to his own home ground once more. Not bad for an old, ailing man like he was supposed to be.

Yet even as he congratulated himself he kept his thoughts from pursuing this vein. For stuck away in a corner of his mind was the knowledge that sometime there would have to come an end to things as they were now. He still had money, but it would run out eventually. Besides, Jon could not be kept in the wilds forever, away from school and isolated from children his own age. Maybe they wouldn't be able to make it through the winter living outdoors in a cave. But his mind held these thoughts in abeyance and did not often let them creep into his consciousness. He lived from day to day trying not to borrow troubles. Best not to cross bridges before you came to them. Maybe something would turn up in the meantime.

Meanwhile, they had a grand time. Daily they swam in some nearby pool, and this proved to be a great pleasure to Benjamin as well as Jon. Clumsy and awkward as he was on land, he found he could float and paddle about as easily as ever in the water. And he relished watching Jon take to the water with all the verve and enthusiasm of a young puppy. The boy had hardly known how to swim at all when they had stepped into the first deep hole they came to, but now he splashed about with gay, confident abandon.

One of the first things they had done was to unwind their gear, cut new poles, and get back to the now partly serious business of catching fish. They worked their way up and down both sides of the creek trying all the promising fishing holes, and they found their luck to be far better than it had been back at the tiny stream in the park. They were usually able to catch all they wanted, and the fresh fish made good eating after so many days of meals from cans and boxes. But Benjamin would not let them get carried away with the sport of the thing into catching more than they could use. He was glad to find this stream had not been fished out, and he didn't aim for it to get that way.

After a few days of resting and fishing and dabbling about in the water, they began to want to strike out farther afield to explore their surroundings. Benjamin was especially anxious to get a closer look at the house and outbuildings. So late one evening they left the creek bottom and made their way across a great wide field to approach the knoll that sloped gently up to the homesite. Benjamin trod joyfully over this span of ground, the earth yielding up a familiarity he could feel through the soles of his feet. This was his own good soil, and he recognized it in his bones and loved it as before. Many a time he'd plowed and sowed and worked this field. Looked as though it had only been used for a hay crop this year though. That was probably about the best a body could do with it now. Benton wasn't a full time farmer anyway. The place was mostly a hobby to him, not the serious business it had been for Benjamin, who had tilled the soil in earnest. But it was hard to make Benjamin's kind of farming pay nowadays, and he was glad that the land was being used, even if only for pasture and hay.

Now they were drawing near to a high fence that marked off the garden plot, and Benjamin squinted his eyes, trying to see through to judge the size and verdure of the patch. It was getting too dark to tell too much about it, but he could make out the tomato vines, all properly staked up, and they looked good, all grown to a nice size. And down at one end of the garden stood a couple of rows of climbing beans that looked mighty nice. They should be bearing heavily about now. Probably Lois Benton was busy canning them as fast as they came on. Then just across the fence from him were some squash vines, and, bending down, he could see a few of the yellowing fruit tucked beneath the great, broad leaves. Yes, it looked like the garden was doing well. There were more weeds in the fence rows than Kate would have allowed, but other than that he couldn't find much to complain about.

Quietly then they crept along the garden fence until they

passed the last tall post and found themselves beside the orchard. The fence dropped to waist-high here, and just a few steps further they came to a gate. Benjamin worried a bit about that gate, for it had always been a squeaky one. When he pressed the latch and gently eased it open without making much noise, certainly nothing that could be heard up at the house. He let out his breath in a sigh of relief, then turned his eyes up to the familiar shapes of the apple trees that loomed overhead. Then he sought out the pear and plum trees, and beyond them the peaches. That one peach off to the left there had never done very well. Seemed like the winters were usually a little too long here for that variety. But when it did bear, the fruit was good. He strolled along between the trees in the little orchard, reaching out to rest his hand in a momentary caress upon the coarse bark of a study trunk, then grasping at a drooping bough that hung heavy with ripening fruit. These were all his trees, once little sprouts that he'd set out years ago. They'd produced a lot of good fruit over the years. It looked like they were still doing so. Tall grass and weeds had grown up pretty rank beneath them, but he guessed that didn't hurt anything except to make the place look a little untidy.

He drew near the edge of the orchard then and stopped to peer out from behind a tree. There stood his house just across the back yard, its shape as familiar to him as that of his own body, and out of its downstairs windows poured a warm, beckoning light. He could almost feel himself returning from evening chores at the barn, eager to bang the kitchen door behind him and settle into the comfort of the shelter within. But it wrenched his heart to let his imagination take him that far, so he turned away, ready to retrace his steps. Just as he started to lift his foot he was startled to feel something nudge him gently across the shins. He teetered as he halted his forward motion and grabbed at Jon to steady himself. Then he looked down to see a great black and white cat turn and make another pass at his legs.

"Why, it's old Pete!" he exclaimed in a loud whisper. As quickly as he could he knelt down beside the close-pressing animal, and as he reached out his gnarled hand to stroke the furry back the cat responded with more vigorous rubbings and the rumbling of a deep-throated purr.

Benjamin chuckled and lifted the cat up to his breast for a quick squeeze, then set him back down again.

"Yessir, it's old Pete!" he repeated, marveling at the discovery.

"Do you know this cat?" Jon asked, bending down beside him to investigate the over-friendly animal.

"Yes. Yes, I sure do. He's my old tomcat. But I don't know what he's doing here. When I got sick, some friends of mine took him to their place to look after him. Took my dog too. But I guess Pete didn't stay. It's funny—they live nearly ten miles away. I don't know how he found his way back."

Jon put out a hesitant hand to touch the cat's head.

"Can I pet him?" he asked.

"Sure," Benjamin encouraged. "He'll let you. He likes all the petting he can get."

More bravely then, Jon extended his caress down the length of the cat's back, and he laughed aloud as the animal moved over to rub against him in response.

"Maybe we'd better be heading back now," Benjamin suggested with an uneasy look toward the house after Jon's mirthful outburst. If they got too noisy playing with the cat they might attract some attention.

"Well—okay," Jon agreed, but he was plainly loath to leave the animal. Yet he stood up, as did Benjamin, and they moved off toward the orchard, passed beneath its trees again, and reached the gate through which they had entered. Gently they eased it open and slipped through, then turned and latched it carefully behind them. But not before the cat slid through between their feet and began to follow them on their way back across the wide field. Sometimes he trailed behind or ranged off to one side, but more often he paraded in front so closely as to hazard their tripping over him.

"He wants to stay right with us, doesn't he?" Jon commented happily.

"Yes, too close," Benjamin grumbled, stepping aside as the cat plopped down and rolled over directly in his path. "He just wants us to notice him, but he's sure making a nuisance of himself."

Thus erractically the trio made their way back to the creek.

There they waded a shallow place to the other side, and the cat, finding a tree that lay across the stream, danced across it to follow them all the way back to their cave. There they built up the fire for light and spent another happy hour playing with him. When Jon went to sleep that night his new-found friend was curled up tight against his breast.

Yet when morning came the cat was gone.

"I wonder why he went away," Jon murmured unhappily as he went to the mouth of the cave and peered about looking for the pet. "We were good to him, and he seemed to like us."

"Oh, he liked us all right. But Pete is an independent old rascal. He comes and goes pretty much as he pleases. That's just the way cats are. He's probably out hunting himself a mouse or something this morning. But he'll come back to see us again, I expect. Whenever he gets the notion."

After Jon had peered wistfully into the woods all day without finding him, the cat suddenly dropped from a nearby rock into the glare of the campfire that evening while they were eating supper.

"Hey, you were right!" Jon shouted. "He did come back. You said he would, and he did!"

"The old beggar knew enough to show up right at meal time too," Benjamin said, pulling a morsel off a catfish carcass he held in his hand. "Here, Pete. There's not much left, but here's a little bite."

"Oh, I wish I had something to feed him," Jon said, "but I've eaten all my fish already."

"Well—you might mix him up some of that powdered milk. He'd like that. Here, stir it up in this little pan."

"Okay!" Eagerly Jon jumped to the task. He dashed down to the creek for some water, then rushed back. "Is he still here?" he called as he neared the cave.

"Yes. Don't worry, he's going to hang around long enough for you to feed him." Benjamin smiled to himself as he watched Jon hastily stir up the milk and set it hopefully in front of the cat. Children needed pets to fuss over. It was good that old Pete had showed up.

"Now, how's that, Pete?" Jon murmured encouragingly.

"Did I get it fixed the way you like it?" He hovered over the animal as Pete took a few tentative sniffs and then began lapping it up.

"Hey, he likes it!" Jon announced gleefully.

"Yes. Always a big milk drinker that one was," Benjamin said. "But of course he used to get it right fresh from the cow. I always gave him a bowl when I finished milking, while it was still warm. He probably thinks this powdered milk is something different."

Different or not, the milk suited Pete well enough, and he lapped it all up, much to Jon's delight.

"He was really hungry, wasn't he?" Jon asked when the cat at last turned away from the pan.

"Well, maybe hunting wasn't very good for him today."

"Do you think he's had enough now?"

"Oh, yes! See how his sides are bulging? He's so full he's about to pop."

"I hope he doesn't have to go hungry very much."

"Oh, it doesn't look to me like he's suffered any. He certainly hasn't gotten thin." Benjamin reached out to feel the cat's back and fondle his ears. "I expect the Bentons are feeding him, and maybe some of the other neighbors too. Pete's been around the neighborhood a long time. A lot of people know him."

"And now we're here to help look after him too."

"Yes. We're here all right. But if we don't get some more groceries pretty soon, we won't have enough to feed ourselves, much less a cat."

"We can always catch fish. And there's some blackberries back there in the woods."

"Yes, but we need more than that. And I know where there is a little grocery store too, just a mile or so from my place. We could get there all right, but I'm afraid that if we went in to buy something we might be recognized."

"Do you know the people that run it?"

"Yes. Well, I used to. But they're getting on in years. I suppose it's possible they've sold out by now. I've never heard of it though, and it looks like somebody would have mentioned it to me if they had."

"Maybe we ought to go have a look and see if they're still there."

"Yes, we can at least do that. We might be able to figure out some way to buy a few groceries."

Late the next afternoon they cleaned up as well as they could and started off to the store. They followed the stream to where it left Benjamin's property, then walked along a fence row that offered the cover of some brush and trees until they came to a wide, paved road. There they paused to reconnoiter before going on.

"This is the main road leading south out of town," Benjamin warned. "Quite a few cars come this way. We'll have to look out for them."

"Which way is the store?" Jon asked.

"Right down there to the left on this side of the road. See, there where that gasoline sign is. It's mainly a filling station really, but they carry quite a good stock of groceries too."

"Well, how shall we get there?"

Benjamin studied the situation for a long moment.

"I think it would be best if we crossed the road and walked down through that pasture. There are quite a few trees we can hide behind if we hear a car coming. Right across from the store there is a big clump of oaks, and we can look things over from there without being seen."

When the road was empty they scurried across the pavement to the opposite side, then made their way unobserved to the cover of the oak grove and ducked down out of sight to watch the comings and goings across the way.

"Looks like old Wyatt is the only one minding the store now," Benjamin murmured at last.

"Who?" asked Jon.

"Wyatt Davis. He's the one who's been pumping the gas. He and Nellie, his wife, have been running this place for a long time."

"They're the ones you know then?"

"Yes," Benjamin said with a sigh, "they sure are. I'd hoped they might at least have hired somebody else to handle the evening business. They used to complain all the time about having to keep such long hours, and they were always looking for help. I thought by now they might have someone."

"Well, then you can't go in. But what about me? Think I should try it?"

"Well—maybe. Tell you what, let's wait until some other customer comes. Then maybe Wyatt will be so busy talking to somebody else that he won't pay much attention to you."

They leaned back against two trees and waited. Five minutes went by. Then ten. Jon was getting restless to try his luck. Every minute or so he fidgeted around to peer out from behind his tree and see if anything was happening. Then at last an old pickup truck rattled into the station, and Jon tensed with readiness to go.

"Wait a minute," Benjamin warned. "Wait until they aren't looking this way!"

"Okay," Jon breathed. He held himself poised another few seconds until Wyatt and the overalled man who had stepped from the pickup turned to examine a stack of used tires that stood at one corner of the station. Then he scooted out from behind a tree and dashed to the fence that separated the pasture from the road. Quickly he wriggled under it. Once upon the road he slowed to a leisurely pace and strolled into the store with scarcely a glance from either of the men.

Once inside he let out a deeply held breath and began a hurried search up and down the aisles. In a few moments he had his arms full of groceries, and he went to the counter and dumped them down beside the cash register. Then he waited, listening as the voices of the two men mumbled gently almost out of hearing, then suddenly grew louder as they moved closer and stepped through the door.

" . . . want to pick up some bread and some bacon too," the farmer was saying as he entered the room.

"Sure. Well, you let me know about the tires. I'll put those two back and save them for you until Saturday anyway." Then seeing the boy waiting at the counter, the old man turned his attention to him. "Got all you want there?" he asked as he moved over to the cash register.

"Yes," Jon replied, keeping his eyes down upon his purchases.

"Okay, I'll ring them right up," Wyatt said, giving the boy only a slightly curious glance as he turned to an ancient cash register. "You're new around here, aren't you?" he continued, punching the prices into the machine and then ripping off the sales slip to tuck it into a paper bag as he dumped the groceries into it. "That'll be four dollars and fifty-seven cents."

"Yes, kinda new," Jon answered, pulling a five-dollar bill from his pocket and handing it over. Still he refused to meet the grocerman's gaze full-faced. About that time the farmer brought his purchases to the register drawing Wyatt's attention once more away from the boy. Jon scooped up his bag of groceries and headed for the door, flashing a triumphant grin toward where he knew Benjamin was hiding as he shoved the screen open and bounded down a couple of steps. But he turned and walked down the road until he was out of sight of the store's occupants before he crossed back over.

"Did you have any trouble?" Benjamin asked as Jon slipped back through the fence to join him.

"No, not much. He thought I was new all right, but he didn't bother me much about it."

"Well, that's a relief. I don't mind telling you I was kind of worried."

"What shall we do now? Head for home?"

"Yes, we'd better hustle before it gets too dark. Then we'll get busy and cook up some of these groceries for our supper."

They made haste carefully and managed to get back to their home territory before the night had gathered too thickly about them. When they walked up to their cave, Pete came trotting out to meet them, rubbing against their legs.

"You didn't tell me to do it," Jon said hesitantly as he drew one particular can out of the bag, "but I bought a can of cat food for Pete. It didn't cost much. It was the cheapest kind they had."

"Oh, that's all right," Benjamin assured him. "I guess we can't let old Pete go hungry while we sit around here stuffing ourselves." In spite of his ready agreement, he wondered if they were spending money on the cat that they might some day be needing for themselves. As usual he refrained from thinking too much about it. They were home now and comfortable and having a good time, quite free from their former oppressions. That was enough for the time being. He would not concern himself further.

So the days slipped by, and they continued to live in their Huckleberry Finn world, reveling in the freedoms of their existence. For a long time no problems arose. Food was plentiful, for fishing and berrying were good, and sometimes they slipped up to the orchard and gathered a few windfall apples and pears that were going to waste. They found some nubbins of corn that the Bentons had tossed aside too, and now and then scavenged for flawed tomatoes that Lois Benton had discarded while picking them for canning. Benjamin was careful not to take anything that the Bentons were harvesting for their own use. Even the leftovers, though, did much to improve their daily fare.

What they couldn't scavenge they bought, and no problems arose there either. After the first visit, old Wyatt paid little attention to Jon other than to take his money and give him change.

With plenty of time to do as they pleased, Benjamin began to find his feet itching to re-explore his whole farm. He wanted to tread his land, to see and feel all of it once more. So each day thereafter they tramped about as much as his strength would allow, sometimes walking through the fields but carefully staying out of view of the house, and sometimes hiking into the hills. Jon seemed to enjoy it as much as he did. With each hill the boy ascended, each view he scanned, each rock he tossed, each tree he climbed, his acquaintance with the farm grew until it almost equalled that of his old friend. And he loved it almost as well.

The golden days were interrupted at last by the first fall rain. For three days they waited out the damp, chilly hours huddled in the cave over the fire. During the cool nights it became apparent to them that they needed to make themselves a warmer bed. So when the weather cleared and turned dry again they busied themselves gathering armloads of dry grass to heap in a great mound at the back of their cave. Then when it was deep enough, they burrowed down in it and covered themselves over with their blanket and plastic sheet and slept warmly once more.

The mornings were staying cool now. Yet though they were not quite as comfortable as before, still they managed well enough, for the little cave with a fire burning at its mouth held a fairly even temperature, and they simply stayed inside longer when the days grew sharp with cold. Usually the midday warmed up to a soft, hazy balm that was pure delight. They roamed the nearby woods, scrounging limbs and branches which they carried back to stack beside their shelter. There should be no problem about firewood, Benjamin guessed, gauging the available supply of downed trees and limbs within their reach.

For a time, they got by well enough. As the season grew colder and wetter, they were more often driven inside the cave, and sometimes the inactivity there did grow tedious, especially for Jon. Still there often came warm days with balmy afternoons when they could fish and dabble about in the water enough to bathe a little and do their laundry. As long as it wasn't raining, even the sharp, crisp days were good for tramping about through the woods.

The days that the rains kept them mostly inside were not totally without their pleasures. While they sat and stared at the fire or looked out upon the dripping world round about they talked. Sometimes Benjamin spun tales of his boyhood. Sometimes he moved up a generation and talked about his own family until Jon grew so well acquainted with Kate and the kids that he almost felt himself to be one of them. Sometimes their conversation grew serious, and they had long theological discussions about life and God. Very gently Benjamin introduced his own faith to the boy and knew that the child was taking it in and considering it. Daily, he prayed for the youngster, for to Benjamin it was a fearful thing to go through life without believing. He wanted better than that for this child. The boy had had little enough to guide and comfort him thus far.

So he told the old tales, the Bible stories he had read and believed since his own childhood, and especially he told about Jesus, the God-man, about how He had walked this earth with love and compassion and healing for all who needed it. He laid out simply the ancient truths—how His coming, His death and His resurrection had meant salvation from sin and the promise of eternal life for believers then, and of how it still brought the same forgiveness and hope to those who trust in Him today. He couldn't be sure, but it seemed to him that some of the child's bitterness drained away.

Yet the boy would never discuss his own family. He listened eagerly to Benjamin's tales, but never told of good times of his own. Had there then been no good times at all? Perhaps none that the sickness and neglect of his parents did not overshadow.

Benjamin kept on with his tales, building a picture for the boy of what a family should be, of how wholesome people lived and worked and played together, of how they sometimes disagreed but never failed to love each other, of how they trusted God and prayed and worshipped and tried to do right. And he told how, when they failed in doing right, they asked forgiveness of God and believed that they received it. He knew that the boy wondered at his stories, both the ancient ones and the personal ones, and pondered whether such things could really be true. What he did not know was that the boy also, having judged much from his old friend, began to think that perhaps they were.

Chapter 10

All continued to go well until the snow came. Even that was fun the first day. It was a light snow, a couple of inches, and Jon frolicked in it, making snowballs as often as his unmittened hands would allow and trying to slide down a little hill on a makeshift sled he concocted from the remains of a cardboard carton he had found and dragged home a few days before. He went to the store to stock up on groceries in case bad weather should continue, and they felt snug and safe when they retired to their cave that evening. The night brought more snow, several inches more, enough to keep them inside most of the next day and make them glad they had a good stack of firewood handy. It had turned snapping cold too. They were snug inside their cave though, and it was still fun to sit safely inside the shelter and look out upon the beauty of the whitened world round about and watch the dwindling snow showers that fell off and on throughout the day.

Another day brought the end of the storm and started things warming up, but it took several more to melt the snow enough to expose here and there brown, wet patches of bare ground. One crisp morning when the thin, crunchy crust looked enticing for tramping around, Benjamin was surprised to find Jon content to remain inside the cave. The boy sat listlessly beside the fire or curled up in the blanket on the bed and lay staring dully at the ceiling. It seemed strange behavior for a kid who had been raring to go when the snow first began.

"Are you feeling all right?" Benjamin questioned him a couple of times. Jon insisted that he was, though he admitted to the second query that maybe he was just a little bit tired.

Benjamin didn't ask for help when he went to carry more wood into the cave. Later, he cautiously made his way alone down to the creek for water. Jon did make a half-hearted gesture towards rising to accompany him when Benjamin picked up the pan and turned to go, but it was apparent that he didn't really want to make the effort, so Benjamin discouraged him.

"Never mind," he told the boy, "I don't need any help. I'm just going to get a pan of water." He was still a little surprised that Jon took him at his word and sank back upon the bed.

It wasn't like him. Something surely was wrong, some ailment of body or spirit. Could he be worried about the prospects of their living out the winter here in these woods with only a cave for shelter? Maybe the snowstorm had frightened him. Hardly seemed likely though. He'd enjoyed it tremendously at first. In fact, he's seemed enthused with everything about their crude mode of living, had even seemed to relish some of the small hardships they'd endured.

Surely it was something else. Perhaps he really was ill, coming down with something or other. With that thought Benjamin grew fearful as he trudged back to the cave entrance with his pan of water. In all his planning he'd never once thought about the possibility of Jon's getting sick. He'd often had to push down concern about whether or not he would be able to hold up, but he'd never doubted that Jon would. He seemed such a sturdy boy in spite of his thin, frail-looking frame. Well, maybe it wasn't anything much. Maybe it would soon pass.

By suppertime that evening, he knew his fears were not groundless. Jon would not, or could not, eat.

"I'm just not hungry," he said at last after he had sat and stared for a long while at the plate of beans and wieners cradled in his lap. "Maybe we can save this till tomorrow, and I can eat it then, huh?"

"Why, of course you don't have to eat it if you don't want it, Jon—either today or tomorrow."

"But I shouldn't waste it when we haven't got too much food left!" the child wailed, and he seemed upset out of all proportion to the problem of a bit of leftover food. He was almost in tears.

"Jon, don't worry about that. I may even eat it myself if I get hungry again pretty soon. And we'll soon be able to get out to the store and get some more groceries. Anyhow, what's more important is why you aren't hungry. Are you feeling bad? Do you think you might be getting sick?"

"No. Just my stomach doesn't feel too good. It doesn't seem to want any food in it."

"Well, then you mustn't be trying to force anything down. Here, why don't you come on back over to the bed and lie down for a while."

Jon set his plate down with relief and crept over to the bed of leaves where he curled up into a tight ball and let Benjamin tuck the blanket snugly around him.

"Just rest now," Benjamin instructed him. "I'll clean up the supper things. You don't need to bother about anything."

The boy lay quietly and after a time drifted off into a light, uneasy slumber. Benjamin puttered about the fire, tending to the simple camp chores, and brewing himself a cup of coffee. Then he sat down, and leaning his back against a smooth patch of rock in the cave's wall, he tried to relax. The sound of Jon's breathing kept him tense and listening, for it grew heavy and labored and was occasionally accompanied by a slight moan. Even the cup of coffee that he now held gingerly to his lips, letting the fragrant vapors flow warmly across his face, failed to give him much comfort. Not while the boy lay restlessly tossing in his bed, seemingly suffering in his sleep.

Twice Benjamin went to the child's side to draw the blanket up once more around him after he had unknowingly flung it aside. Each time he returned to sit by the fire and keep it blazing high with fresh-fed wood. If the boy were ailing it wouldn't do to let him get chilled, and he had begun to feel certain that Jon was indeed ill. He'd sat beside too many childhood sickbeds not to recognize the symptoms. Halfway through the night the child seemed to sink into a deeper, quieter slumber, and Benjamin allowed himself to think that perhaps the worst was over. He stoked the fire with some good keeping wood and turned toward the bed, gently easing himself down beside the boy so as not to disturb him. Jon half-roused to realize that Benjamin was there and turned to curl up against him for warmth and comfort.

"Are you cold, Jon?" Benjamin asked, drawing the child's body snugly against his own.

"No, not now that you're here," Jon murmured, and he drifted off again to sleep.

Benjamin lay quietly so as not to further disturb the boy, and then just as he too was about to let his weariness carry him off to sleep he became aware that the small body nestled against him seemed very warm, probably from a fever. But though he worried himself back awake for a few minutes, he knew there was nothing more he could do about it tonight. Best let the child get his sleep out if he could. Maybe he'd be better by morning.

Benjamin knew Jon was worse the moment he wakened to feel the child's hand flung over against his face. It was very hot. He was startled to immediate alertness and raised up on one elbow to lay his hand upon the boy's forehead, feeling for a fever. No doubt about it, the boy was burning up.

When Benjamin slipped out of the bed, the child began to tremble with a chill. Benjamin tucked the blanket snugly around him and piled on every spare garment he had, then hurried to the smoldering fire and began urging it to greater heat with dry, fast-burning wood. He turned back to the bed to find Jon's eyes anxiously upon him, his body still shaking with the chill.

Benjamin lay back down beside Jon to add the warmth of his own body until the fire should better heat the cave. As he drew the small body up to his breast, he was shocked again at the heat of the fever. Gratefully Jon snuggled against him and lay there with his teeth chattering until gradually the trembling eased to intermittent tremors.

"Feel a little better now?" Benjamin asked.

"Yes." Jon's voice was feeble, but Benjamin could feel his head nodding in his arms.

"Well, I'm going to try getting up again. I need to put some more wood on the fire. It's getting warm in here now. Maybe you won't get so cold this time when I leave."

"Okay." Jon curled up into a ball when Benjamin drew away, and again Benjamin tucked the bedding firmly about him. Then he returned to the fire and heaped on wood again until it roared.

"It's going good now," he said with satisfaction, and, picking up the saucepan, he nerved himself for the sharp cold outside and plunged out in his shirtsleeves to get snow for water. When he had filled his pan he hurried back to the cave and gratefully hovered as close over the fire as he could bear, turning himself about to warm first his front side and then his back. He placed the pan beside the fire to heat, then got out the skillet and began spreading strips of bacon in it. All the while he could feel the child's eyes, listless and suffering, following his every move.

"Do you feel like eating a little something this morning?" he asked.

"No. I'm still not hungry."

"How about trying a little toast and a cup of tea?" Toast and tea—that had been Kate's invariable offering to anyone on the puny side, and it had always seemed to go down well with a sick child if anything would.

"No, I couldn't eat any toast."

"Well, how about just some tea then? You ought to try to get some fluid down, I think."

"Well—okay. I'll try it."

"Good. I'll have it ready in a jiffy."

Benjamin bustled about getting a tea bag to dangle into a cup, then pouring in the water when it got hot and watching to see that the tea steeped just long enough. It made him feel a little better to be doing something for the boy. Maybe a good cup of tea would perk him up.

It didn't. Benjamin was alarmed to see how weak Jon had grown when he struggled into a sitting position. The effort that it took to stay upright and hold the steaming cup seemed to set off another spell of trembling. When the boy got down a few sips of tea and handed the cup back to him, he took it without argument.

"That's all I can hold now," Jon said, and with a sigh he sank back upon the bed. He closed his eyes and seemed to drift off into a half-slumber from which he stirred and moaned softly from time to time. He seemed to be resting, so Benjamin left him alone and tried to keep himself busy with camp chores, for he needed to do something to keep his mind off the big problem that was rearing before him. If the boy were badly sick—what would he do? He couldn't just let the child lie out here in a cave and suffer. If it were anything serious, that is. But it might be just a little cold coming on. Children could get awfully sick sometimes over some minor complaint, and then they'd bounce right back from it in a day or so. He hoped this was something like that. Probably it was. Probably the fever would break pretty soon, and Jon would wake up hungry and raring to go again. "God, let it be," he prayed.

Jon did wake up halfway through the morning, but he was still burning with fever. He flung the covers aside and sat up, looking around almost as if he were surprised at his surroundings.

"What's the matter, Jon?" Benjamin asked, frightened by the strange wildness in the child's eyes.

"Nothing. I don't know—I'm too hot."

Benjamin laid his palm against the side of the boy's flushed face and was dismayed at the heat he found there.

"I'm afraid you've got a pretty high fever, Jon," he said.

"Yes. I'm too hot. Too hot." The boy got to his knees and started to move away from the bed. "Awful thirsty too," he muttered.

"Don't get up. I'll get you a drink. Do you want some more of that tea you drank this morning?"

"No, just a drink of water. Cool water."

"All right. Just wait right there, and I'll go down to the creek and get some fresh."

He waited and watched a moment to be sure Jon had settled back down, and then he left the cave and made his way cautiously to the creek bank. It was safe enough to make the walk now. Already the sun had warmed the earth enough to melt the crust of ice except for a few places that still stood in the deep shade of a rock or a tree, and he could easily avoid those spots. He knelt on a grassy spot and dipped up a full pot of water, and he shivered in spite of the sunshine upon his back when his hand splashed down into the liquid cold. Yet the day brightened and sparkled around him as he climbed back up the hill, and he was cheered. It was going to be a nice day. Going to warm up, it looked like. Probably Jon would feel better when he saw how nice it was outside. Maybe then he'd get over this little puny spell and everything would get back to normal.

Thus he encouraged himself, and when he got back inside the cave he also tried to encourage Jon. He spoke brightly to the boy as he poured a cup of the cold water, and he wet a handkerchief to bathe the child's face when he had lain back down upon the bed. Funny he hadn't thought to do this before. Kate had always laid a wet washcloth across a child's forehead to cool a fever. He felt better having something to do for the boy, and he sat beside him a long time, lifting the cloth every few minutes to wet and cool it afresh before laying it gently back down.

The boy lay quietly and tried to be eased by the ministrations. Yet as the day moved on into afternoon Benjamin grew increasingly fearful. Jon was not really getting better. In fact, he seemed to be worse. The fever held high, and the chilling began again.

Benjamin was caught in an agony of indecision. Surely Jon's illness wasn't serious. Surely it was just one of those things— viruses they called them nowadays—that he'd get over all right. Probably by tomorrow he'd be lots better. A good night's sleep should do wonders for him, make him good as new again.

Suppose it didn't, though? Suppose this did turn out to be something serious, something that needed doctoring. Benjamin couldn't let the boy lie out here in this cave and suffer—and maybe worse.

What could he do? If he went for help he'd give everything away. There would be no way to do it without letting people know where he was and where the boy was and what they'd been up to. It would be the end of everything for them. They'd be separated no doubt, and he knew where he'd end up—right back in the Home. How could he stand that?

And Jon, what of him? His folks mustn't have him back, but Benjamin wouldn't be able to keep them from it. The police would stick him back in the Home, and he wouldn't have any more say about what became of Jon. Maybe it was better for Jon to be sick, to take his chances on getting well out here in the woods, than to have to have to go back to his parents. For a moment he tried to believe that this was true, but he could not quite do it. No, the most important thing was for Jon to get well. Then maybe something could be worked out. He'd tell the police all about how Jon had been treated at home. They would do something. There were laws about such things. Surely they wouldn't give him back to his folks. They'd find someplace else for him. Yes, he thought it would work out like that.

But he wouldn't get to be with Jon any more. He'd be trapped in that Home again, sure as the world. He might even end up in jail. Maybe they'd accuse him of kidnapping. He guessed it could look like that. Whatever they did, it was sure to be something unpleasant. He'd be shut up somewhere or other. He could hardly bear to think about it. Not when he'd tasted the joy of roaming the fields and woods again as he had these weeks.

No, he didn't want to go back, and he knew Jon didn't want to either. He'd better settle down and not do anything rash. Any moment the boy might start to get better. There were lots of daylight hours yet, and he had plenty of time to wait before deciding what to do. No need to go rushing off in a dither.

He calmed himself and set himself to patiently wait, performing what little ministries he could for the child, trying to feel that he was easing him.

The day wore on, slowly but inexorably. As the afternoon passed he began to peer out every few minutes to see how far the sun had slid down into the western sky. Each time, he would turn back to see if the boy were showing any improvement yet. Sometimes Jon would try to rouse himself a bit in response to his friend's concern, but it was only a pseudo-liveliness, and Benjamin could tell it. At last he looked out upon the sun and saw it sunk so low that he knew he could wait no longer. It would soon be dark, and he couldn't risk making the walk out then. He must either go now or wait until morning. He had to decide.

Benjamin stepped outside the cave and paced a few steps in a circle in an agony of indecision, inwardly crying to God for guidance. Then he turned and faced the hovering sun once more and made up his mind. He would go. No matter what might come to them as a result, nothing mattered quite so much as for the boy to get well. Yes, he must go.

He stepped back inside the cave and went over to crouch down beside the bed. He gazed at the closed eyes in the small, silently suffering face a moment and then softly spoke the boy's name.

"Jon. Jon, can you wake up and listen to me a minute?"

The child's eyes slowly opened and peered up into his.

"Jon, I'm going to build up the fire real good, and then I'm going to leave you alone here for a little while. I think I'd better go get us some help."

"Help?" the child's voice quavered in return. "What for?"

"To get you to a doctor, Jon. I'm afraid you're getting pretty sick, and there's nothing more I can do for you. I think you need a doctor."

"No! No! Then everybody will find out where we are!"

"Yes." Benjamin was silent for a moment, wishing that somehow even yet he could decide it wasn't really necessary to give themselves away. If Jon would just insist against it, or claim he was feeling better—but no, he mustn't even consider such possibilities. He knew what he must do.

"I'm sorry, Jon," he said, reaching down to stroke the boy's hair back from his forehead. "I don't want us to have to leave here either. But I don't know what else to do. There just isn't anything else now. When you're as sick as this you need a doctor."

"But I don't want to go back home," the child's voice wailed to a quivering treble. "Please don't make me," he pleaded. And from his fever and distress the tears began to flow.

"No, no," Benjamin hastened to assure, "I didn't mean you had to go back home. I'll try to fix it so you won't have to go there."

"Well, where else would I go?"

"I don't know for sure. But we'll work out something. We'll find a place." He paused, knowing there was little assurance for the child in these vague promises. But then he hurried on. "You might have to go to the hospital right at first until you get well. After that I'll try to see to it that you have some place to go besides home. I promise you, Jon, I'll do my very best to arrange it."

"But I don't want to have some place else to go. I want to stay with you!"

"Yes—well, I don't know—" A vision of Jon sharing his room at the nursing home rose up to flaunt its impossibility in his face. "I don't think I can promise you that—

"You see? That's why I don't want you to go!"

Benjamin sat silent, groaning inwardly. What more could he say? He had no real comfort for the boy.

Then the child continued his pleading. "Besides, what will happen to you? Where will you go?"

"I don't know—for sure. But don't worry about that, Jon. I'll be all right, wherever I end up."

"Even back in that old Home?"

"Yes, even there. Anything's better than having you here sick."

"Well, I don't think so!"

"Jon, I do have to go." The tone in his voice settled the argument.

So the boy left off his pleadings and turned away as Benjamin went about the business of building up the fire with some good keeping wood. Then the old man spoke one more time.

"I'm leaving now, Jon. It shouldn't be too long before somebody comes. The Bentons are good people. They'll help me get you to a doctor. So just lie quiet and rest until someone comes to get you."

Jon didn't say anything for a moment, but he finally gave in and nodded his head with a mumbled, "Okay."

"Are you warm enough?"

"Yes."

"All right then. I'd better get going." Benjamin paused and bent down to lay his hand on the boy's shoulder. "Take it easy, and I'll see you later."

"Will you?" Jon's voice burst out in doubt and anger.

"Will I what?" Benjamin asked, not understanding the child's anguish.

"Will you see me later? Ever again?"

"Why, Jon, of course."

The old man turned to go then for he couldn't let the boy read the anguish and doubt in his face. His own grief he thrust aside by concentrating on the path ahead and the task he faced in following it alone.

The biggest hurdle, getting across the creek unaided, was coming up right away. He knew where he wanted to try it. There was a place a little ways upstream where a tree had fallen across the stream, and he felt sure that it would offer enough hand-holds to get him across. The water was shallow there, and if he did fall at least he wouldn't drown as long as he could get hold of something to pull himself back to his feet. Jon would have danced across on that thin, springing trunk, but Benjamin wasn't about to try that. He'd do well to make it wading.

He stopped to roll up his pants legs when he reached the spot and took off his shoes, knotting a lace of each to sling them across his shoulders. Then he stood for a moment looking down into the icy water, just thinking about stepping into it raised a crop of goose bumps on his body. But the crossing had to be made. He reached out to find a firm spot on which to plant his cane, and with his other hand he grasped a tree limb and started across.

He made it halfway without difficulty. He was even congratulating himself on his steadiness as he drew near the opposite bank, for he could see that only a couple more steps would put him on dry land once more. He had counted his success too soon—a rock teetered beneath his foot and sent him into a paroxysm of weaving and clutching as he fought to retain his balance.

He did manage not to fall, but when he had gotten his feet squarely under him again he felt the weight of the shoes missing from his shoulder. He had lost them! He turned as quickly as he dared and looked about in the water. At first he saw nothing, but then he spotted a glimpse of brown leather back under the tree. Yes, there they were, swept back and hung on a tiny branch. He bent towards them, but he could not reach either shoe. He'd have to climb over the tree to reach them, and he wasn't about to try that. Maybe though he could get out onto the bank and go around the tree to get at them from the other side.

Cautiously he maneuvered himself out of the water and up onto solid ground again, then circled around the top branches which had fanned out in an arc upon the bank where they had fallen. When he reached the stream bed again he crept carefully into the edge of the water and swept his eyes back and forth, searching for another glimpse of his shoes. Everything looked different from this side, and the water was darkening with the approach of evening, but at last he spotted the limb on which they were caught. It was still out of his reach, so he took a tentative step towards it. But his foot plunged into a deeper hole, and the water surged up to his knees as he staggered about in the unexpected depth. Then when he poked the stream bed before him with his cane, he found there was another dropoff just ahead. Must be a sizable hole there. He'd better not try to wade any farther out into that.

But he wasn't far from his shoes now. He could see them bobbing about just beneath the surface. They were still tied together. If he could just get hold of one of them the other would have to follow.

Holding to a limb with one hand and stretching as far as he could with the other, he still could not reach the shoes. He was at least a couple of feet short. He needed something to extend his reach. So, straightening for a moment, he reversed his cane in his left hand and holding it by its rubber-tipped end he stretched out once more toward the shoes.

With the cane he could reach them! Easily! Happily he thought his problem solved, and he began to lower the cane to snag them with its crook. When he brought it down it bumped against the little branch that tenuously held the shoes, and the twig bobbed down and up and lost its hold on them. They slid away, tumbled slowly end over end, and then disappeared from view as he made a frantic thrust after them with his cane. He thrashed the cane about in the water trying to locate them, but it was no use. They were gone. Perhaps not far, but gone neverthe-less. Finally he realized it, gave up, and turned to make his way disconsolately back to the bank. He stepped out of the water and stomped angrily about, wiping the mud and water off his feet in the chill, crumpled grass.

"Doggone it," he muttered as he chastised himself. "How could I have done such a stupid thing?" He should have known that throwing those shoes over his shoulder wasn't a safe way to carry them. If only he had tied them to his belt. Or thrown them on across ahead of him. Anything but just tossing them loose across his shoulder like that. He should have known better!

When he rolled his pants legs down the chill of the wet fab-ric, now soaked to his thighs, turned his thoughts away from his anger to the discomfort he was suffering. He felt the cold sharp-ly as a rising wind pressed the wet trousers against his legs, and already his feet hurt just from going this little distance barefoot. He had a long way to walk to get to the house. All that way he had to go now without his shoes. It was a painful prospect.

Self-pity arising from his predicament for a moment sapped his strength. Seemed the odds were going awfully strong against him on making this trip. Maybe it wasn't meant for him to go after all. Maybe this accident meant he just shouldn't try to do it. He thought for a moment about going back to camp and standing by the hot fire to warm himself and dry his pants. It was an alluring picture. But he couldn't give up that easily. He was no quitter; he'd make it up to the house somehow, shoes or no shoes.

"I ran around all over the countryside barefoot when I was a kid," he muttered to himself, "I ought to be able to go that little way without my shoes."

But his feet were tender now, and the first few steps made him wince and hesitate. Then enough of his anger returned to stiffen his resolve, and he ignored the stabs of pain and began plodding his way stoically across the field, turning off his feel-ings from the miseries of his battered feet and the cold flappings of his trousers about his legs. He wouldn't let himself be both-ered by such things now. Time enough for that when he had got safely up to the house and had sent someone back for Jon. He picked out a tall pine that he recognized as marking one corner of the barn lot and blundered steadily toward it.

Dusk had begun to settle heavily now, for he had lost a good deal of time getting across the creek and trying to recover his shoes. He tried holding his cane out in front of him to get warning of approaching obstacles, and sometimes this worked. But sometimes it didn't, and twice he fell. The first tumble only threw him to his hands and knees, but the second thumped him flat onto the ground and jarred him through and through. Yet when he had collected his senses and begun to stir gingerly he found himself still intact. Both arms and legs worked fine, and as soon as the hurt subsided a little he was able to struggle back to his feet and move on. He felt something warm trickle down his cheek, and he touched his hand to the spot to discover a bit of red wetness. He'd felt something jab at the side of his face when he hit. Must have gotten a scratch that was bleeding a little. It didn't hurt though, surely didn't amount to anything.

In fact, he wasn't hurting much now anywhere. His feet were so numbed by the cold that he felt no pain no matter what he stepped on. The stabs and scrapes went all unheeded. So he crept slowly across the wide fields, concentrating on heading in the right direction and not letting himself stop. Somehow he felt that if he paused to rest he wouldn't be able to get going again.

Finally, almost to his surprise, the great pine he had been using for a goal loomed overhead and he found himself bumping against the orchard gate. He grasped at a couple of pickets and leaned on it for a moment, then forced his fingers to begin searching for the latch. It was on the other side of the gate, but he remembered exactly where it was and quickly located it. Getting it undone was another matter. His fingers were stiff and unfeeling, and they fumbled badly at the task, refusing to do his bidding. He worked and worked at it, but it didn't budge.

"Come on now—open—open," he muttered, using both hands to manipulate the device. But still it stuck. Silently he faulted himself for not having replaced that latch long ago. It always had been a little hard to work. But never quite so stubborn as this. It just wouldn't open for him.

He soon gave up his efforts and stood clinging to the gate

trying to figure out what to do next. He could have wept with frustration. If he couldn't get in here he would have to find another way. But he didn't want to find another way. He didn't want to have to struggle any more. He was tired, so tired. He had a feeling his strength was going fast and he couldn't wait too much longer to finish his journey and get up to the house. He thought about following the fence around the garden, but it was too far to another gate that way. He'd have to go around to the front yard.

He looked up toward where the bright squares of the farmhouse's lighted windows beckoned to him. All that light and warmth and comfort waited so near. He almost forgot that the Bentons would be within the house. It seemed to him that if he could get to the kitchen door and open it he'd find Kate waiting inside.

If only he could get through this gate. Angered by its hindrance, he suddenly lifted his cane and reached over the top of the gate to hack at the offending latch. He didn't really hope to open it this way. He was simply punishing it.

"If I can't open it maybe I can bust it," he muttered, and he banged away at the resisting device, striking the cane against it again and again. He thought he was dealing hard blows, for he swung the weapon with all his might. But in actuality his efforts were feeble and in little danger of damaging the gate.

Yet suddenly he noticed a loosening as the gate rattled more freely with each blow. He stopped his pounding and leaned over to examine the latch. He could hardly tell what his fingers were doing, but as he pushed and shoved at the device he did sense that it loosed its hold and moved back from its catch. All that pounding must have shaken something loose. He pressed his weight against the gate and it opened. It shrieked loudly as it bent upon its hinges, and at first this frightened him. Someone might hear and come to find him. Then he remembered that it didn't matter if he were found. That was what he had come for, to get in touch with the Bentons and get some help for Jon.

He thought it strange that although he wasn't hurting anywhere at all now he seemed to wobble in a most disconcerting manner as he walked through the orchard. He made his way from tree to tree, stopping to hold to one for a moment until he had the next one firmly in his sight, then cautiously loosening his grasp and stumbling off again. Thus he made his way haltingly until he finally left the last tree behind and stood before another gate. This one opened into the back yard and was the last barrier he had to get through. Between this gate and the beaconing kitchen windows was nothing but a wide expanse of lawn and the back porch. He pressed gently against the gate, and to his surprise it swung open at his touch.

He was home free now. Nothing could stop him. He felt fine. He didn't even seem to be tired any more. He lurched forward, but for some reason those beckoning kitchen lights kept moving off to one side or the other. Each time that happened he had to stop and turn himself until he got oriented to them again.

At last he found himself at the back porch. Laboriously he lifted himself up one step at a time, resting a little after each upward heave. With the third one he found himself on the level again. He took a few deep breaths, then aimed carefully at the kitchen door. He couldn't see it, for it was very dark between the two bright windows, but he knew it was centered squarely between them, and he shoved off in that direction.

He hit with a bump and waited a minute to see if anyone would come. He thought he could hear voices inside and someone stirring about. The door didn't open, though, so he leaned back from it a bit and began pounding on it with his fist. He thought he was making a fearful racket, but actually he produced only feeble thumps. Still, it was enough to attract attention, for he heard footsteps coming nearer, and then the doorknob began to rattle. At the same time the porch light came on, and he was dazed by the flooding light.

Then the kitchen door flew open, and the bright house light further blinded him. He stood there, blinking and wondering at the gasp and little scream that came from Lois Benton. He'd forgotten about the scratch on his face. He didn't know that blood was running down the side of his face and dribbling onto his collar. He didn't know that his hair stood on end and that his eyes peered at her with an unfocused stare. He didn't realize when Tom Benton grabbed his arm and drew him inside that his feet left bloody tracks with each step. He couldn't understand why both Tom and Lois seemed excited and upset as they steered him to the nearest chair.

"It is Mr. Wright, isn't it?" Lois asked. Benjamin heard her, but her voice seemed to come from way off in the distance somewhere.

"Yes." Tom sounded a little closer. "Yes, it's him all right. But how do you suppose he got here?"

Benjamin couldn't seem to get his own words started. He just listened and smiled a bit as they fluttered around him, bringing a pan of water to bathe his feet and a damp cloth to wash his face. Then Lois handed him a cup of coffee, and after he had drunk a few swallows he got his voice started. He told them, over and over, that there was a sick boy waiting for help down in one of the caves beside the creek. At first they didn't believe him. They seemed to think he was imagining things. But he kept insisting and calling Jon by name. Finally he was relieved to see Tom pull on his boots and coat and walk out the back door with a flashlight in his hand. He was going to look. Good. That was all Benjamin needed to worry about. Everything would be taken care of now.

So he didn't protest at all when Lois bandaged his feet and led him gently to the living room couch. He lay down at her bidding and let her tuck a blanket about him. He rested there contentedly, for he was satisfied that he had done well. Jon would be taken care of. There might be other things to worry about later, but right now all was well.

Chapter 11

Benjamin stirred and stretched a little as the early daylight laid a tentative hand upon his face. He was surprised upon first reaching consciousness, as he had been for a good many mornings now, to feel a pillow under his head and the sharp smoothness of sheets against his arms and legs. No more did he waken to find himself nestled in a rustling bed of leaves. He was back in the Home, and he awoke to the feel of fresh bedding about him and the sight of a wall and window on one side and a white curtain that hung between his bed and that of his roommate on the other.

He was always disappointed when his eyes first opened upon the scene, but he was trying hard to be reconciled to it, and each time he firmly put his disappointment away. What was done was done. This morning he turned toward the window, as he usually did, reminding himself that the sun shone the same here as it did out in the woods and that the ever-changing scene of the sky was just as available. He looked to an upper corner of his window where the etchings of a maple branch moved with gentle dignity up and down against the sheen of a faintly gray sky. Must be a little breeze out there. Looked like it was going to be a nice day though. Good. Gave him something to look forward to.

It seemed there was something else he was looking forward to today too. Oh, yes, Stephen was coming. It would be good to visit with him. He'd been here a couple of times since Benjamin got back, and he'd been awfully nice about everything, not scolding or fussing over him like Janet did. Of course Janet meant well. He knew that. She was motivated by a real concern for him. But her frettings did get on his nerves just the same. Steve would be calm and friendly instead, keeping any criticism he might have to himself. Yes, Stephen's visit would be something to look forward to. Just thinking about it made him anxious to start the day.

It was good to be able to get up and do for himself again. For a while he hadn't been able to. His feet had been so cut and bruised from that long walk across the fields that he'd only been able to get about in a wheelchair. He glanced over at that abhorrent contraption still ready and waiting in a corner of his room. He was glad he didn't have to fool with that thing any more.

He finished dressing quietly so as not to disturb his roommate, then stepped softly around the neighboring bed and went toward the door, glancing down at the gently snoring form as he passed. Poor old Herbert, he wouldn't be getting up for breakfast. He was past being able to get to the dining room for meals. They'd be bringing him a tray pretty soon. Benjamin was thankful he was in better shape than that.

Gently he closed the door behind him and, grasping the hand rail, started down the hall. Looked like he was going to be one of the first ones on hand for breakfast as usual. He'd always been an early riser and wasn't likely to change his ways now. Well, no matter. There'd be someone along to visit with pretty soon, and he could sit and talk while he waited for his meal. He always looked forward to breakfast, though he felt he should have been out doing his chores before he ate. Well, those days were gone forever. He'd given in to that. He was trying to take things as they came and not get too worked up if they didn't go to suit him. It was better to think about the things going on around him that he did like—such as the good coffee smell that freshened his senses as he stepped into the dining room.

"Good morning, Mr. Wright," came a cheery greeting from Irma, one of the kitchen help who was busy setting tables. "You're up bright and early this morning."

"Yes, well, there's nothing very exciting about lying around in bed. It's better down here where I can at least smell the food."

"Well, if you consider the smell of oatmeal and poached

eggs all that exciting," she replied, laughing.

"Hungry as I am, that does sound pretty exciting."

"Well, we're almost ready to start serving. Just try to hold out for a few more minutes." She paused in her conversation, punctuating the silence with a clatter of silver as she spread eating utensils upon a table. "What do you hear from your little friend these days?" she continued then.

"Oh, not much. But he's out of the hospital and in a foster home now. Staying with some people over in the east end of town. I haven't met them, but I think they must be nice folks. Jon called me on the phone right after he went to live with them, and he said they were being real good to him."

"Well, I sure hope so. That little kid sure deserves a break after all the trouble he's been through."

"Yes. Yes, he sure does," Benjamin fervently agreed. And as Irma hurried back into the kitchen he sat and thought about Jon, missing him so much that for a time he scarcely noticed when others began to gather at the table around him. He spooned down his oatmeal almost without tasting it, and then he sat and sipped his coffee with his mind re-doing the events of their exodus from the wilderness. He was hazy about some of it, especially what had happened that first night. But he did remember Tom Benton pounding on the back door after a time and Lois scurrying to open it. Then Tom had stepped inside with Jon blanket-wrapped and cradled in his arms. There'd been excited, anxious talk then and much fussing over both strays until they were warmly bundled and packed into the car for the drive to town. Then there had come the blur of the white hospital scenes. Benjamin had been kept there only overnight, but it had been a trying time for him with doctors poking at him and police talking to him. He'd been glad to see the police though, had even asked for them. He still had to try to keep Jon safe, and now there was no other way to do it but through them.

He'd told them, over and over as long as they would listen, that the boy had been mistreated at home and it wasn't safe to return him there. Evidently they'd believed him, for the doctors had begun to investigate Jon's condition as soon as he was over the worst of his illness, and they'd found plenty of corroborating evidence. Several previous head injuries had been found to have taken place, and there were numerous scars indicative of other hurts that would be hard to account for by usual childhood accidents. A couple of broken bones had even showed up. Funny Jon had never mentioned those to him. Still, the boy had never seemed to want to talk much about his sufferings. He seemed strangely ashamed of them. Then too, some of these things might have happened when he was too small to remember.

It still was almost more than Benjamin could bear to think of the little tyke being tormented like that. For a moment he felt a surge of rebellion wedge its way up into his faith, but he quickly took himself in hand and, rising abruptly from the table, shook his doubts from him as he hurried out of the dining room and stumbled repenting down the hall. After all, God's love had been well-proven. That was what his faith was all about. "God so loved the world . . . " Yes, he believed that.

He reached his room and hurried through the door to his chair, then sank down into it with scarcely a nod for the aide who was standing beside Herbert's bed helping him with his breakfast. He didn't mean to be rude, but he was so wound up in his thoughts that he didn't want to break into them even with friendly conversation. He took a magazine from his bedside table and spread it across his lap, bowing his head over it to seem to be reading while he thought and prayed. It was a small subterfuge, one of several that he had learned to use when he wanted to get a little privacy to do some thinking. Such tricks were necessary around this place. Especially now that Herbert had failed so badly that he needed a lot of attention. Kept a constant parade of people coming and going in the room. Benjamin had found ways of keeping to himself when he needed to.

He sat and pondered awhile until his mood settled, and then in a quiet moment without realizing it he dozed off to sleep. He was still nodding there in his chair when Stephen entered the room and bent down to gently touch his shoulder.

Benjamin bobbed his head with a start to see Stephen's good, square face smiling down at him.

"Why, hello, son," Benjamin greeted him. "Didn't expect you so early."

"Well, Jeannie and I have got some socializing to do tonight, so I thought I'd come on down this morning and see you, and then I'll have to leave fairly early this afternoon. We'll have plenty of time to visit though. I thought we might go out to lunch somewhere at noon. If you'd like to, that is. Think you can bear to tear yourself away from the dining room here for one meal?"

"I sure can! No trouble at all!"

"Your feet doing all right?"

"Oh, sure. I get around fine. Been walking outside the last couple of days. I did two laps around the grounds yesterday."

"Sounds like quite a bit. Still, nothing to what you did when you hiked all the way out to the farm, I guess." Stephen allowed a small smile to quiver at the corners of his mouth. "Did you really walk all that way, Dad? Just you and the boy? No rides at all?"

"Nope, not a one. We walked every step. But we did it a little bit at a time. It took a while."

"I don't wonder. That's a far piece." Benjamin was gratified to hear a note of wonder and admiration creep into his son's voice. "Took a lot of gumption, I know. But, Dad—you were taking some chances."

"Aw—I'm not near as sickly as everybody makes me out to be. I got along just fine."

"That's not what the doctor says, Dad."

"Well—he doesn't know everything."

"No, but—we do have to assume that he knows something about your condition. And he sure thinks you shouldn't have been out gallivanting around the countryside by yourself. He says you got along remarkably well, but you were pressing your luck. He doesn't think you should try to live alone."

"Huh!" Ire at the traitorous advice of the doctor exploded from Benjamin. "A lot he knows! I did it, didn't I? I don't know as I need that—that quack—anyway."

"Now, Dad, Dr. Barnes isn't a quack. You know that."

Benjamin did know it, but he didn't want to admit it, so he

clamped his mouth shut and sat unspeaking for an uncomfortable moment as they sparred silently.

Then Stephen sighed and spoke again.

"Tell me, Dad—why did you leave in the first place? Is it so bad here?" He hesitated visibly, then went on to the next question. "Did they mistreat you—or anything like that?"

"No. They were good to me. At least they mostly tried to be."

"Well, then?"

Benjamin shifted about in his chair as he tried to collect his thoughts to explain.

"I don't know if I can tell you," he began hesitantly. "So you can understand anyway. It's just that—I got to feeling so cooped up in here. There's people around you all the time. You can't get away from them. They're always telling you when to do things. You can't decide anything for yourself. Everything has to be their way. It's—it's a prison, that's what it is. I had to get out and—just look over the land again. The hills and the trees and the crops—everything. You know."

Stephen slowly nodded his head. "Yes, I see."

Benjamin doubted that he really did. It was hard to explain the strong urgings that had driven him away from the Home last spring. The need to leave had been overwhelming. He tried to analyze it a bit more in his own mind, hoping perhaps to better lay it out before his son. But then Stephen pressed on, and further explanations were left behind.

"Well, I guess the thing to be thinking about now," he said, "is what to do about it."

Benjamin's heart leaped. It sounded as if Stephen had a plan in mind. Some way to get him out of here. He didn't want to appear too anxious, but he couldn't help leaning forward a little with eagerness to hear.

"First of all, Dad, you've got to consider your alternatives. Then decide. We—Janet, Mary and I—we've talked it over the last few days. I called Mary and talked to her over the phone. And we'd like you to help figure out what is the best thing for you to do. I'm sorry that we didn't take the trouble to find out how you felt about staying here. But of course right at first you were too sick to decide anything, and later on—we just didn't realize."

"I know, I know. It's all right."

"Now, as to what can be done. As I said, I've talked to Mary on the phone a couple of times. She's willing to help financially, and she's well able to—you know that—but she feels that it might not work out too well to have you move right in with her and Ben. You know how they live, in that apartment in the middle of the city, and they travel around so much because of Ben's work that it would be hard for you—for things—to be properly looked after. Mary might have to stay home all the time instead of going along with Ben.

"Oh, I wouldn't want that. No, I wouldn't want to be any bother to them."

"Well, I hardly thought it would be the best solution."

"No. I don't think I could stand living in that city anyway. I've never been able to understand why Mary likes it there. She always used to enjoy the farm so much—when she was little, anyway. She's changed, I guess."

"Yes. Well, that happens." Stephen squirmed in his chair a bit, then got back to the subject. "But that leaves Janet—and me. Janet is willing to take you in with them. And she will have a spare room next fall when Jim goes away to college. She even said they could manage to crowd up somehow between now and then if you wanted to move in right away. I don't know how you'd feel about it—living with Janet—trying to get along with her."

Yes, Benjamin thought, that would take some doing. He and Janet hadn't gotten along so well of recent years. She was a good woman, and he loved her dearly. But she was a managing woman, and if there were anything he didn't need it was more managing. It would be like jumping from the frying pan into the fire, for it would be harder to take such bossing from his own daughter than from the nurses and aides around here. The time he spent around Janet would probably best be rationed to brief visits rather than a full time living arrangement. If he had to get mad at somebody for pestering him, better the people at the Home than her.

"Well, I don't know, son," he began with some embarrassment. "I hate to say that I couldn't get along with Janet. Maybe I could. But it would be—difficult. I doubt if it would work out very well."

"Yes. Well, then there's me—and Jeannie."

Jeannie. Yes, there was Jeannie to think about. He liked Stephen's wife, and he thought they'd get along fine. But she had been losing her sight for the last couple of years and now was almost blind. She had problems enough of her own without his adding to them. Oh, she managed very well. She and Stephen lived happy, almost normal lives in spite of her handicap. But Benjamin knew it wasn't always easy for her. He certainly didn't want to add himself to her list of burdens.

"I don't think Jeannie needs me underfoot," he said. "She has enough to worry with already."

"I've already talked to her about it, and she says it's okay with her if you want to come in with us. She said we could clear out the sewing room for you. It wouldn't matter. She hardly ever tries to sew any more."

"Well, it's mighty generous of her. And you too. But I couldn't do it, Steve. I'd feel like a burden. I *would* be a burden—I couldn't help it. And I couldn't stand that."

Silently Stephen accepted his verdict, and although he didn't say so Benjamin knew that he was relieved. They both sat unspeaking for another long moment, and then Stephen spoke again.

"Well, Dad, where does that leave us?"

"Not much of anyplace, I guess," Benjamin replied with disappointment and disgust. He hated being a problem to his family, hated creating a difficulty that they felt they had to try to work out. He could imagine their getting together to discuss the topic of what to do about poor old Dad, and he didn't care much for the picture. "But I don't see why I have to stay with any of you," he protested with a touch of rebellion edging into his voice.

"Then what else could you do?" Stephen asked. He paused, then went on slowly and carefully. "Dad, do you really think you could live alone?"

"Well, I did, didn't I?"

"But you had the boy with you. Didn't he help some?"

"Yes. Yes, he did." His voice dropped to a murmur as he remembered. Jon had helped him a great deal.

"And, Dad—suppose you'd had another attack somewhere out there in the woods. The boy couldn't have taken care of that, you know."

"Yes—well, I didn't aim to do that. I was feeling good. All that time I felt real good. I wasn't about to have an attack of anything!"

"But, Dad!" Exasperation came into Stephen's voice. "You couldn't possibly know that—" He caught his words and held them back for a moment, then went on again. "Well, that doesn't matter anymore. What does matter is what we're—what you're going to do now."

He waited a bit, but Benjamin had nothing further to offer, so he went ahead and forced out more words.

"How are you feeling now? Are you as strong as you were before you—came back here?"

Benjamin stirred uneasily. "Well, no, not quite. That last night kind of did me in. But I'm getting better. I'll be all right."

"But still—I do think you need some help, Dad. I just can't see your trying to live alone any more."

"Humph!"

"Well, now, just listen a minute. I know you don't like the idea of living in this place. But how would it be if you stayed here just through the week—Monday through Friday—and then came out to our place for the weekends? I'd be home then and could help Jeannie any time she needed it. We could have a good visit and maybe get out for a picnic now and then when the weather's nice. Maybe even drive out to the farm once in a while. The Bentons told us to bring you out for a visit any time you'd like to come. If Jeannie and I were tied up some weekends, maybe you could go spend a couple of days with Janet instead, just once in a while." Stephen paused and watched his father's face closely. "Do you think something like that would make things better for you?"

"Wouldn't it be a lot of trouble for you to have to come and get me every week and then bring me back?"

"No, no. I often have business here to take care of, and I can usually schedule that for a Friday afternoon. Then after I'm through I can pick you up and head on home. Jeannie likes to come along with me to shop now and then too. And, after all, it isn't so terribly far, only about a forty-minute drive. We can manage it."

"Well, I don't mind telling you it would help. I think I could stand it here a lot better through the week if I knew I was going to get away over the weekend. But I sure don't want to be a burden to anybody."

"Oh, Dad, you know you wouldn't be a burden to Jeannie and me. We always enjoy having you around."

"All the same, I want you to promise that you won't go to a lot of extra trouble for me. Any weekend you're too busy to come get me, just say so. I know you sometimes have a lot of work to do, and I don't want to get in the way. Besides, you and Jeannie need a weekend to yourselves sometimes."

"All right, I'll let you know any time we can't manage it."

"I guess I could go to Janet's now and then." Benjamin gave a small, wry smile. "I could stand a little ordering around for just a weekend, I suppose."

"Okay, then. We'll try it. Sounds to me like everything should work out fine—if you can be content to stay here through the week."

"Well—I'll manage."

They sat in silence for a few moments then as each contemplated his share of the arrangement. Benjamin hoped they wouldn't get tired of him after a while and quit coming to get him. He didn't think it would turn out like that. Stephen was a good man. He'd hold to his end of the bargain. It would be a great pleasure to Benjamin to be around his son that much. They'd always gotten on well, although over the years Stephen had gotten so wrapped up in his business and family affairs that his parents hadn't seen very much of him. Benjamin suspected that Stephen was feeling a bit guilty about that now, but no matter. He would certainly make up for it by having Benjamin underfoot almost every weekend.

Benjamin told himself he must try hard not to be a bother and get on their nerves. He wouldn't want to spoil this arrangement. It wasn't a solution he'd have chosen; he'd still have to spend an awful lot of time around the Home. But he guessed he'd have to give in to doing it their way. His family seemed determined to have him looked after. And he had to admit to himself that his recent adventures did seem to have taken some of the starch out of him. He just didn't have much get up and go left at all. But he might get better. And if he did get better—a lot better—well, he'd just have to wait and see. In the meantime he would try to go along.

"I told you I talked to Mary on the phone, didn't I?" Stephen's voice broke into his thoughts then. "Well, she said she'd plan to come back for a visit next summer. Sometime in June probably."

"That'll be nice," Benjamin said, the calm in his voice concealing the leap in his heart. Dear Mary, the baby of the family and the one he'd secretly doted on the most, yet the one fledgling that had strayed farthest from the nest. "It's been a while since we've seen her, hasn't it?"

"Yes. Not since Mom's funeral."

That was right, Benjamin thought; she had come back for the funeral. He remembered how surprised he'd been then to see how much she'd aged. He still thought of her as about seventeen, the way she looked when she graduated from high school. And when he went for several years at a time without seeing her he was always surprised to find her a middle-aged, slightly-graying woman. Well, it would be awfully good to see her again, no matter how she looked. And June wasn't so terribly far away. It would give him something to look forward to the next few months.

"Well, do you think we ought to go see about getting us some dinner now?" Stephen asked.

"Sure, sounds good."

Benjamin began the struggle to rise from his chair, but he had sat so long that his joints had stiffened and didn't want to bend into new positions. He gave a couple of futile heaves, and then Stephen bent down to help him. He was irritated by the gesture and felt an impulse to jerk away from Stephen's helping hand. He almost did. Instead, he forced himself to give in to accepting the aid and then was angry for feeling so contrary about it. Why was it so hard to accept help from his children? It had been easier with Jon, because he had been able to help him in return. There was nothing he could do for Stephen any more.

The sturdy, stalwart image he'd always presented to his sons was hard to give up. But he'd been over all this before. He couldn't help being old and feeble. His age was not a weakness to feel guilty about. There were many ways of being a man. Without resentment, he let Stephen hold to his arm and steer him a bit as they made their way down the hall and out to the car. They managed some easy, trivial man-talk as they drove across town to the eating place Stephen had picked out.

It was a good dinner, and Benjamin enjoyed it. It had been a long time since he'd sat down to a feed like this in a good restaurant. A far cry from the meals he and Jon had thrown together out in the wilds. There were, after all, some compensations to being back in civilization. Yet in his heart he knew that he would have traded the restaurant food in a minute for some fried fish and pork and beans and maybe a potato baked in the coals of a campfire that he and Jon had kindled together. An ache gathered in the center of his chest as he pictured the two of them huddled over their fireplace stirring up a simple meal and bantering friendly conversation back and forth. He could see Jon's eyes sparkle in accompaniment to the snapping fire below, and was pained that he would never know that scene again.

That was the way of things. He was an old man; he'd lived long enough to know that nothing good—or bad—lasted forever in this old world. He was glad for the time he and Jon had had together. One of the best times of his life it had been. It would make for many good memories to cling to when the Home began to get him down. Now he mustn't let his wishful thinking spoil the nice dinner Stephen had arranged for him. He pushed the pain away as well as he could and dug into the steak that a smiling waitress had placed before him.

They ate long and well and then lingered over their coffee cups for more conversation. It was the best visit they'd had in a

long time. He was going to enjoy being around Steve on weekends if they could have time for talks like this. Maybe they
would really get acquainted again. After all, Stephen's kids were
pretty much grown and on their own now. Steve must surely be
free of some of his former responsibilities. He might have more
time now to sit and chew the fat with his old dad. Benjamin
hoped it would turn out that way. He'd look forward to finding
out next weekend.

The meal hour passed in good companionship, and at last
they rose, satiated and content, and made their way leisurely
back to the car. Stephen drove them around a bit, just to pro-
long the visit and do a little sight-seeing before they returned to
the Home. Finally, his time was up, and he pulled once more
into the circle drive that swept past the entrance of the institu-
tion.

"Well, I'm sorry to have to leave you so soon, Dad. But you
know how it is."

"Sure, I know. Well, thanks for the dinner. It was real
good."

"Oh, you're welcome. Glad you enjoyed it." Then Stephen
started up quickly from his seat, for his father had begun to
struggle with the door on his side. "Here, let me come around
and give you a hand," he said, and, hopping out of the car, he
hurried to the other side. "I'll walk down to your room with
you," he suggested as he helped Benjamin lift himself out of the
car seat.

"No, no. I can manage fine. You'd better get going or you'll
be late getting home."

Stephen glanced up to see one of the aides eyeing them
through the glass door. She saw them coming; she'd lend a hand
if it were needed.

"Okay, then," he said, escorting his father safely to the
doorway. "We'll see you Friday evening. Be ready about 5:30.
And don't let them feed you dinner around here. Jeannie'll have
something good cooked up for us when we get home."

A few moments later, Benjamin crossed the threshold into
his own room. He stopped with a sigh just inside the doorway
and looked around. It was clean and neat, but small and dreary

just the same. Poor old Herbert there, he sure wasn't much company. If only he could see Jon again. Just thinking about the little tyke brought him a pang of loneliness. He wondered what the youngster was doing today, right now. Somehow, his yearning seemed to draw his eyes to a sheet of paper that was propped against the water pitcher on his bedside table. He hurried over to get a closer look, for it looked like—yes, it was Jon's handwriting! With a wrench of his heart he grabbed up the paper and with trembling hands adjusted it to the right distance for reading.

"Dear Benjamin,

I came to see you, but you were not here. My Aunt Julia brought me. She has come to get me to go live with her. We are leaving today. We are going to fly in an airplane. I have never been on an airplane before. I wish I could see you. I will write you a letter soon.

Goodbye,
Jon."

So. It had happened. They had taken Jon away from him, so far that he would never see him again. He stumbled over to his chair and sat down, holding the letter carefully so as not to wrinkle it or drop it. And when he was settled he read it again, his eyes caressing each wobbly turn of the boy's handwriting until they blurred from the tears that came. He didn't even try to stop them. He was so grieved at his loss that he didn't care whether anyone saw him or not.

Then when the worst of it was over he told himself all the comforting things he could think of. Wasn't this, after all, what he had wanted at one time, someone in the family to take Jon and look after him? He remembered when he'd proposed that very thing. If this aunt were good to him it would probably be a much better arrangement for the boy than a foster home. He'd hoped that he might be able to see Jon now and then, but if he had to sacrifice that for the sake of the child's having a real home—well, so be it.

He sure wished, though, that he'd been here today to tell Jon goodbye. He'd only seen him once since they left the woods. While still in the hospital Jon had asked about him so much that finally arrangements had been made to get Benjamin up there. Janet had managed that, bless her. She and her husband, Tom, had loaded him into their station wagon, carted along the wheelchair, and upon arrival at the hospital had maneuvered him up the elevator and down the hall to Jon's room. The boy had been weak still from his illness but quite able to visit with him, and they'd had a quiet but glad reunion. Though he hadn't been allowed a very long stay it was enough to reassure each that the other was all right.

They had parted happily, expecting to have a chance to get together again soon. Yet for some reason it hadn't worked out that way. Benjamin wondered about that. Perhaps Jon's father or the authorities or the foster home people hadn't allowed it. Maybe they thought he was a bad influence on the boy, encouraging him to run away and get into trouble. He didn't know. And it didn't really matter now, not with Jon so far away that they couldn't possibly see each other anyway.

He tried to turn his mind away from the boy and onto thoughts less distressing. Like looking forward to his next weekend with Stephen. He had to get five days through here at the Home before then. That was a lot of time. He sighed heavily as he contemplated the prospect. He'd manage somehow.

Benjamin portioned each day into segments for the little activities he could manage, and he waded determinedly through each one of them until he saw the tedium of the day come to an end with an aide's final flipping of the light switch in his room at night. When the weekend visit did come, it was good, though Stephen wondered a bit at his father's frequent air of distraction. Seemed to have his mind off somewhere else a good deal of the time.

Benjamin returned to the Home and made it through another five days there, and the pain of losing Jon subsided a little. Yet he knew some of it would always be there. He'd had experience with these things before. Didn't he still miss Timothy, even after all these years? And Kate—oh, how he yearned after her every day. Mary, too. She'd been away for so long that he missed her almost the same. And now Jon. A thousand pictures rose up to confront his memory. Their first meeting, their fishing expeditions, their adventures in the park and their shopping trip into the city. Then their flight and the long, toilsome journey across the rolling countryside. The hot day in the barn and the long, comforting day in the church. The last awful hill they'd climbed. The farm and the creek and the home they'd made in the cave upon its banks.

In each picture there came to him a sun-tanned, shaggy-headed boy, his dark eyes holding back secrets and mysteries while his shy but ready grin gave out a plea for friendship. With gratitude Benjamin remembered the child's willingness to be a companion to an old man. Jon was a good boy—a real good boy.

So with his memories and his putterings about the Home he got through another week and once again spent two days with Stephen and Jeannie. Again, it was a happy time. He tried hard not to be any bother to Jeannie, and he thought she really was glad to have him around Saturday, for that day Stephen had to be gone most of the time, and Benjamin was company for her. Then Sunday Stephen had plenty of leisure, and they had a quiet, comfortable time. Stephen told him to bring along his suit next week and they'd all go to church. Benjamin wasn't so keen about the big, fancy church Stephen and Jeannie attended, but it would be better than not going at all. Then in the middle of the afternoon Janet and her husband came by for a couple of hours, and the visit turned into a regular family reunion. When at last it was time for Stephen to drive his father back to the Home, Jeannie decided to go along too, and they took a long way around so they could stop on the way for hamburgers and chocolate shakes.

It was all good, and Benjamin was content when Stephen left him at the door to his room. He'd be able to make it now, he thought. He didn't like the Home, but he could stand it if he could have these pleasant weekends to look forward to. If only Jon were around to get in on them too! He'd sure like for Jon to meet Stephen and Jeannie and Janet and Tom, to get to be around them a bit. It would be good for him, give him some more adult friends. There was no use thinking about that. It couldn't happen with Jon way off somewhere.

Just as he settled in his chair and began thinking about the boy, wondering what he was doing and how he was getting along, he heard a light rap on the door, and Helen, one of his favorite aides, stuck her head inside.

"Did you find your mail?" she asked. "A letter came to you yesterday, and I put it on the stand there."

"Why, no, I hadn't noticed it. Thanks for telling me."

She was just as quickly gone, and Benjamin turned to the stand, wondering. Who would have written him? Mary perhaps. But when he found the envelope and looked at it his heart leaped, for there slanting in boyish printing across the envelope was Jon's handwriting. Yet the first page he opened was taken up with a small, womanly script.

> "Dear Mr. Wright,
>
> Jon has told me so much about you that I feel that I know you, even though we have never met. Since I'm sure you are much interested in his welfare, I thought I'd write a note along with Jon's letter to let you know that we are looking after him to the best of our ability and will continue to do so as long as it is necessary.
>
> Jon's mother is presently undergoing psychiatric treatment, and at this time it is uncertain whether she will ever be able to undertake his care again. My husband and I have no children of our own, so we are enjoying very much having him here with us. We have been hearing from Jon the things you have taught him about God and the Bible stories you have told, and we can tell that you have laid a good foundation, one upon which we will certainly continue to build.
>
> I'm sorry we missed you the day we came by. Jon wanted very much to get to tell you goodbye, but we had to catch a flight late in the afternoon and didn't have time to wait.
>
> Thank you again for your interest in Jon and your concern for him.
>
> Sincerely,
> Julia Hedgepeth"

"Well," Benjamin murmured with a sigh of relief, "Jon's aunt sounds like she's okay. Sounds like he's in a loving Christian home."

Then he quickly laid her letter aside, for he wanted to get

into the blocky printing that bore Jon's message to him. He smoothed the creases from the page and held it up to read.

"Dear Benjamin,

I've been here at my aunt's house over a week now. They have been real nice so far. I have to go to school here now. The school is so far away that I have to ride a bus, but that is okay. I don't mind it. I go to church, too. My aunt and uncle go every Sunday I think. The church is close to their house. We can walk to it. It is a big church and I would rather go to your little church but I will probably get used to this one. My uncle likes to go fishing like I do. He is going to take me with him when the weather gets warmer. You should see his fancy fishing poles. I have been wondering what happened to our poles and stuff at the cave. Do you think everything is still there? I would like to go back and see. Do you think Pete is getting enough to eat without us there to feed him? I hope he is all right. I hope you are all right too. I sure would like to see you. I might get to come back to visit Dad next summer. I may see Mother too. If I do get to come back I will come to see you. Will you write me a letter? I hope so.

Yours truly,
Jon"

"Well, now," Benjamin breathed the words softly and happily, "that's quite a letter for a little fellow. Quite a letter." And he quickly turned to the drawer in his bedside table and began rummaging around in it for an envelope and writing paper. Jon wanted to hear from him, and he was certainly going to oblige.

He sat on the edge of the bed, and, drawing his bedside table near, he laid the paper on it and bent over to write.

"Dear Jon,

I was very happy to receive your good letter. I'm glad that things are going well for you. It sounds like your aunt and uncle are real fine people. I hope you will enjoy living with them.

I am getting along okay. Stephen has been coming to get me to spend the weekends at his place, so I don't have to stay here at the Home every single day. It isn't so bad that way.

I expect all our camping stuff is still at the cave, but I don't know for sure. The Bentons could have gathered it up by now

I guess. I sure do miss being out there with you, but perhaps it is just as well that things turned out as they did. Now you can have a good home with your aunt and uncle. I hope you weren't too far behind when you started back to school. I'm sure you are smart enough to catch up.

Don't worry about old Pete. The Bentons came to see me a few days ago, and they said he was still hanging around. They said they would feed him. They are glad to have him around the barn to catch mice.

Well, Jon, I hope you will be as good a boy for your aunt and uncle as you were with me. I am sure you will. I am glad you are going to church with them and hope you will keep on. Also I hope you will work hard at school. I am real proud of you and know you will do well.

I miss you very much, but it won't be too long until summer comes and then perhaps I will get to see you. In the meantime, I hope you will keep writing to me, and I will write to you. That way we can keep in touch. I will be anxious to hear about all the things you are doing. Write soon.

Your friend,
Benjamin"